Thomas Godfrey

Juvenile Poems on Various Subjects

Thomas Godfrey

Juvenile Poems on Various Subjects

ISBN/EAN: 9783337376109

Printed in Europe, USA, Canada, Australia, Japan

Cover: Foto ©Andreas Hilbeck / pixelio.de

More available books at **www.hansebooks.com**

JUVENILE POEMS

VARIOUS SUBJECTS.

WITH THE

PRINCE OF PARTHIA,

· A

T R A G E D Y.

BY THE LATE

M: *THOMAS GODFREY*, Jun!

of P H I L A D E L P H I A.

To which is prefixed,

Some ACCOUNT of the *AUTHOR* and his *WRITINGS*.

Poeta nascitur non fit. HOR.

P H I L A D E L P H I A,
Printed by H E N R Y M I L L E R, ·in Second-Street.
M DCC LXV.

Some ACCOUNT

OF THE

AUTHOR and his WRITINGS.

AS it is probable that this Collection of Poems may fall into the hands of some who are unacquainted with what were the circumstances of the Author, it may not be improper to annex a short Account of him; which, perhaps, may not only gratify the curiosity of such, but assist them in forming a judgment of his natural talent for poetry.

Mr. THOMAS GODFREY, the Author of the following Poems, was born in Philadelphia, in the year 1736. His Father, who was of the same name, was a Glazier by trade, and likewise a Citizen of Philadelphia. A person, whose great natural capacity for Mathematics, has occasioned his name to be known in the learned world: being (as has been heretofore shewn by undeniable * evidences) the original and real inventor of the very useful and famous Sea-Quadrant which has been called HADLEY's.

---

* The Authors of the American Magazine for July and August 1758, have taken much generous pains to do justice to old Mr. GODFREY's memory, and have published an original letter of his to the Royal Society, which does not appear to have been taken any notice of in their transactions, and also two letters of JAMES LOGAN, Esq; which fully prove that the first invention of this Quadrant was undoubtedly Mr. GODFREY's; and that he had formed

He

He died when his Son was very young, and left him to the care of his Relations, by whom he was placed to an English school, and there received † " a common education in his mother tongue ; and with-
" out any other advantage than *that*, a natural genius, and an atten-
" tive perufal of the works of our English Poets, he foon exhibited
" to the world the ftrongeft proofs of poetical capacity. "

It is not to be wondered, therefore, that in the early period of life, he fhould feel fuch a warm impulfe for thofe elegant arts for which nature had formed him. For, befides having a fine ear for Mufic, and an eager propenfity to Poetry, we are told, that, when very young, he difcovered a ftrong inclination to Painting, and was very defirous of being bred to that profeflion. " But thofe who had

---

his plan of it as early as the year 1730. " How he came to be deprived of the honour of
" this invention (fay the writers in the Magazine) may be made a queftion by fome. We
" anfwer, that Mr. GODFREY fent the inftrument to be tried at fea, by an acquaintance of
" his, an ingenious navigator. in a voyage to Jamaica, who fhewed it to a Captain of a fhip
" (faid to be a relation of Mr. HADLEY's juft going to England ; by which means it came
" to the knowledge of Mr. HADLEY, tho', perhaps, without his being told the name of the
" real inventor. This fact is fufficiently known to fundry feamen and others, yet alive in
" Philadelphia "
In fhort, after publifhing the above-mentioned letters. together with Mr. GODFREY's firft
draught of his *Octant*, or *Quadrant* commonly fo called, they conclude thus, " For our part,
" we have no hefitation in pronouncing Mr. GODFREY the real and original inventor of this
" famous and ufeful inftrument. " At the fame time they fpeak with great refpect of Mr.
HADLEY, acknowledging, " That tho' there was fufficient reafon to conclude he was not the
" firft inventor of this inftrument, yet he had great merit in the improvement of it. and that
" his fame in the learned world could fuffer no diminution from the juftice done to Mr. GOD-
" FREY, of whofe name, perhaps, he had never been told. "

† All the quotations, relative to the Author of thefe Poems, are taken from the account publifhed in the American Magazine.

" the

" the charge of him, not having the fame honourable idea either of
" the profeffion or its utility which he had, croffed him in that defire.
" After fome time he was put to a Watch-maker, an ingenious man,
" in this city, but ftill the mufes and graces, poetry and painting
" ftole his attention." He devoted therefore all his private hours to
the cultivation of his parts, and toward the expiration of his time he
compofed thofe performances that were publifhed, with fo much favourable notice, in the American Magazine.

At length he quitted the bufinefs of watch-making, and got himfelf
recommended to a Lieutenant's commiffion in the Pennfylvania forces,
raifed in the year 1758, for the expedition againft Fort Du Qu fne;
in which ftation he continued till the campaign was over, when the
Provincial troops were difbanded.

The fucceeding fpring he had an offer made him of being fettled
as a factor in North-Carolina, and, being unemployed, he accepted
of the propofal, and prefently embarked for that place, where he continued upwards of three years. At Carolina it was, that he finifhed
the Dramatic Poem, called, *The Prince of Parthia*, as appears by a
letter of his, to a Gentleman in this city; dated, as early as, Novem-
ber 17th, 1759; which was received after the manufcript of it. " By
the laft veffel from this place," fays he, " I fent you the copy of a
Tragedy I finifhed here, and defired your intereft in bringing it on
the ftage; I have not yet heard of the veffel's arrival, and believe if fhe
is fafe, it will be too late for the Company now in Philadelphia."——
So that he was but about twenty-two years of age when this dramatic
piece was completed.

Mr.

Mr. GODFREY, on the death of his employer, left Carolina, and returned to Philadelphia; but finding nothing offer, that was advantageous, at his return here, he determined to make another voyage abroad; and, accordingly, procured fome fmall commiffions, and went, as a fuper-cargo, to the Ifland of New-Providence, where he was for fome months, but met with no great encouragment. From New-Providence, (led, as it were, by fome fad fatality) he failed, once more, to North-Carolina. Where in a few weeks after his arrival, he was unexpectedly fummoned to pay the debt of nature, and death put a fudden ftop to his earthly wanderings, by hurrying him, off this fhadowy ftate, into a boundlefs eternity.——

He happened, one very hot day, to take a ride into the Country, and, not being much ufed to this exercife, and of a corpulent habit of body, it was imagined the heat overcame him; for the night following he was feized with a violent vomiting and malignant fever; which continued feven or eight days, and at 10 o'Clock, A. M. on the third of Auguft, 1763; put a period to his life, in the 27th year of his age.

Thus haftily was fnatch'd off, in the prime of manhood, this very promifing genius, beloved, and lamented, by all who knew him. What is here prefented to the public, is a collection of thofe fweet effufions which flowed with a noble wildnefs from his elevated foul. Free and unpremeditated he fung, unfkill'd in any precepts, but what were infufed into him by nature, his divine tutorefs. The Public muft judge, whether, from thefe youthful emanations he does not appear to have been animated with the genuine poetic flame.——But whatever defert he may be allowed as a Poet, it will be render'd ftill confpicious by his character as a man. His fweet amiable difpofition, his integrity of heart, his engaging modefty and diffidence of manners, his fervent and difinterefted love for his friends, endeared him to all thofe who fhared his acquaintance, and have flamped the image of him, in indelible characters, on the hearts of his more intimate friends.

Mr. GODFREY was firft made known to the public by the learned Authors of the American Magazine; who feemed pleafed in having an opportunity to acquaint the world with his modeft merit, and of doing all the juftice in their power, both to our Author, and his Father alfo, as was obferv'd above. " Nature, fay they, feems not " to have defigned the Father for a greater Mathematician, than fhe " has the fon for a Poet. The former, was, perhaps, one of the moft " fingular Phænomena that ever appeared in the learned world. For " without the leaft advantages of education, almoft intuitively, and " in a manner entirely his own, he had made himfelf mafter of the " abftrufeft parts of Mathematics and Aftronomy. Juft fo it is with " the Son."———

The firft of our Author's pieces that was publifhed in the Magazine was, the *Invitation*, with the following note : " This little poem was fent to us by an unknown hand, and feems dated as an original; if it be fo, we think it does honour to our city." A little while after, an *Ode* on *Friendfhip*, an *Ode* on *Wine*, and a *Night-Piece* of our Author, made their appearance in the fame periodical work. The *Ode* on *Wine*, fay the Authors, " is wrote with much poetic warmth." " Thefe pieces" continue they, " and fome others of his, fell into " our hands by accident, foon after the appearance of the *Invitation*, " which was found among the reft; and we reckon it one of the " higheft inftances of good fortune that has befallen us, during " the

" the period of our Magazine: that we have had an opportunity of
" making known to the world fo much merit, we mean in confidera-
" tion of h's circumftances and means of improvement." Thefe de-
tached pieces made his name known, and gained him a confiderable deal
of credit; they were reprinted fometime after in the Englifh Magazines.

In the year 1762 was publifhed *The Court of Fancy.* The Authors
of the Magazine, it feems, had feen it before it was finifhed; for we
find this favourable account of it in their literary compilement. " What
" will place him high in the lifts of *Poets* (when it fhall have re-
" ceived his laft hand) is a Poem of confiderable length called *The
" Court of Fancy*; in managing which he fhines in all the fpirit of
" true creative Poetry."

The next year after this, made its appearance in the Pennfylvania
Gazette, that nervous and noble fong of triumph called *Victory*, which
was the laft of our Author's pieces that was publifhed.

The editor will not prefume to anticipate the judgment of the
public on thofe other pieces in this collection, which now make their
firft appearance in print; were it, indeed, proper for him, the ftrong
paffion which he bore to the perfon of the Author, and ftill extends
to his memory, has, he acknowledges, precluded him from being a fuit-
able judge of the merit of thefe Poems.

He would only beg leave, therefore, to remark of the Tragedy of
the *Prince of Parthia*——That it is the firft effay which our Province,
or perhaps this Continent, has, as yet, publicly exhibited of Dramatic
Compofition—and, that there is poffibly fome merit even in endeavouring to overcome noble difficulties, though we fhould happen to
afpire after a flight beyond our years.

" In great attempts 'tis glorious e'en to fall."

That

The Author's youth, when this piece was compofed, his difadvantages in refpect of education, the defultory life he was compelled to lead—and, the arduous nature of the tafk—all confpire to caft a veil over every fault, and to heighten every grace and beauty, which the judicious reader may perceive in perufing it; and induce him to conclude that, even as it ftands, it is no inconfiderable effort towards one of the fublimeft fpecies of Poetry, and no mean inftance of the Author's ftrong inherent genius, unaided as he was by the rules of inftruction.

After what has been faid, fhould any little inaccuracies appear in this collection, it cannot be doubted, but the generous critic, will favour them with an indulgent eye—Inftead of halting at a verbal error, he will be pleafed to fee natural genius ftruggling over all obftacles, and foaring, by ftarts, into the brighteft tracts of Poefy. What might we not have expected, from thefe fair promifes of our Author, had he arrived to a feafon of maturity? More * efpecially had he been nurtured by the foftering hand of art?—For furely in thefe firft fruits,

---

* The reader may, perhaps, obferve that fome of Mr. GODFREY's later performances, are not quite fo correct as fome of his earlier pieces, publifh'd in this collection. The reafon is, that before the publication of the latter, he always fubmitted them to fome of his judicious friends, who made feveral corrections in the diction, grammar and placing the accents; in which laft Article having no rule but his own ear, he is fometimes faulty in his pofthumous and more unfinifhed pieces. Some of thefe blemifhes the Editor has endeavoured to amend; fome he finds have ftill efcaped his notice, for want of due time, from other neceffary engagements, to attend to a more thorough revifal of the fheets; and fome others he thought it would be taking too great liberty to meddle with. The Reader will, perhaps, not blame him for this when he finds, by the *Poftfcript*, that it was occafioned by the fine and ingenious remarks of one of the firft pens among us.

The feveral Pieces in the Magazine, paffed to the Public thro' the hands of the Gentleman who has done the Publifher the honour to favour him with his comment on thefe Poems; and who drew up the Account both of the Father and Son in the Magazine; concluding his Account of the latter with the following generous and moving expreffions—" We hope," fays he, " our " readers will not think this Account too particular, when we are endeavouring to do that " juftice to the genius of a Son of THOMAS GODFREY, which his own genius never had " while it could be of fervice to him."

b

which

which are but as the buddings of his genius, are apparent the seeds of that *divida vis enimi*, which has always characterized the *Poet*; and, in this light, it is hoped they will be received by a candid reader, notwithstanding there may be found in them some trivial faults: for as Mr. Pope judiciously sings,——

> A perfect judge will read each work of wit
> With the same spirit that its Author writ,
> Survey the *Whole*, nor seek slight faults to find
> Where nature moves and rapture warms the mind;——

Mr. Godfrey and his Father, we apprehend, may be ranked among the *natural curiosities* of Pennsylvania; for tho' neither of them had much of human learning, yet by the peculiar felicity of their natural endowments, each of them were enabled, tho' in different ways, to raise themselves to honour in the learned world. It would, therefore, be

---

Young Mr. Godfrey always retained the most grateful sense of favours confered on him, and particularly of the kind notice taken of his Juvenile Pieces by this Gentleman, as well as the share he took in recommending him to a commission in the Provincial service.

About this time also, the same Gentleman, from the pleasure that attends the introducing rising merit into the world, took an opportunity of making known the name of Mr. West; almost literally foretelling, in the following remarkable paragraph, the universal fame which that celebrated *Painter* has since acquired in *Italy*, and is daily acquiring in *England*, perhaps, beyond any other person of his profession of the present age.

Speaking of a small Poem on a Lady's portrait, the Writer says—" We communicate it " with particular pleasure, as the *Lady* who sat, the *Painter* who guided the pencil, and the " *Poet* who so well describes the whole, are all *Natives* of this Province. We are glad of an " opportunity of making known to the world the name of so extraordinary a genius as Mr. West. " He was born in Chester County in this Province, and without the assistance of any Master, " has acquired such a delicacy and correctness of expression in his paintings, joined to such a " laudable thirst of improvement, that we are persuaded, when he shall have more experience " and proper opportunities of viewing the works of able masters, he will become truly emi- " nent in his profession."——Thus we find that this Gentleman's conclusions were drawn from an exact and intelligent observance of the vigorous faculties of these natural genius's; and had our Poet lived, to have received equal advantages in his way, no doubt he would have verified all that his aforesaid friend predicted of him.

matter

matter of great concernment fhould fuch fingular genius's "neglected bloom and neglected die," without any friendly hand to tranfmit their names to pofterity. Nor let any one think that the foul is enervated by a love for the polite arts—no;

" The Mufe's track, where e'er fhe roves,

" Glory purfue, and gen'rous fhame,

" Th' unconquerable mind, and freedom's holy flame." GREY.

A late Writer excellently obferves, that it is doing fome fervice to human Society, *to amufe innocently*; and they know very little of human nature, who think it can bear to be always employed either in the exercife of its duties, or in high and important meditations.—Thofe arts, therefore, that inftruct as well as entertain *innocently*, furely, in fome meafure, deferve our attention; and they who excel in them, the notice of the Public. Confidered purely in a political fenfe, the works of genius are, of all others, the cheapeft entertainments. Never was there a ftate, however barbarous and ignorant, that did not glory in her men of ingenuity; and fuch were never wanting in any ftate, where proper incitements were offered for ftudy and labour.

Our Author's death happening fo foon after he arrived to man's eftate, has occafioned but few anecdotes worthy to be remarked, in this fhort account of him. A relation of the moft material, the Publifher has endeavoured, with as much brevity as poffible, to prefent to the view of the reader; neither did the Author's fudden exit from the ftage of life, admit of any leifure to think of his Poetry. The manufcript pieces, therefore, were left in their primitive form, and they fortunately falling into the hands of a Gentleman, a friend of the Author, at the place where he died, were kindly tranfmitted to this City. The prefent publication was undertaken at the motion, and under the countenance of

fome

some Gentlemen here, of incontestable taste and judgment. The sense the editor has of his own inabilities and inexperience, would have long enough prevented him from venturing on such a task, had he expected any other hand would have offered. But he finds that friendship can excite to difficulties, though the object of its flame is translated into another state of existence; and a desire to please the *Worthy*, prevail, even to the exposing one's self to the sentence of the public. In classing the several pieces, he has studied to place them in such a manner as might yield the best entertainment to the reader, and to suppress those, which, he thought, were not proper for publication—And far be it from him, to repent of the trouble he has had in revising, and transcribing for the Press these posthumous Poems of his friend, when he finds sundry of the first names among us, for virtue, learning and politeness, in his list of subscribers. Happy shall he think himself, if what he has done shall be approved of by those, who have done him the honour to encourage this Work! and thrice happy, if, in this attempt to commemorate his friend, he shall please those, under whose more immediate patronage he would shelter himself, and whose plaudit he prefers as the most valuable reward!

He begs leave to return his thanks to those gentlemen who have been assistant in promoting the subscriptions, and forwarding this undertaking, which, being entered on from the most disinterested views, he was the more readily emboldened to apply to his friends for their aid.

And now it only remains for him to bespeak the candour of the public in behalf of this collection, which, as it is the first of the kind that this Province has produced, and the last legacy of one of her youthful sons, the editor cannot doubt, that it will be received with that good-nature and abatement of rigour, which the Editor's early years alone can justify him in hoping, will be extended to himself.

N. EVANS.

POSTSCRIPT.

IN a note to the foregoing Account, it was observed that some of Mr. GODFREY's Posthumous Pieces are less finished than his earlier performances; and the reader will not wonder at this when he considers the sudden manner in which it pleased the Supreme Wisdom to call him from this earthly stage. It is probable too, as he left his pieces in various hands, and some of them were frequently transcribed, that several mistakes might have been made this way. The Publisher when he first entered on this undertaking, intended to have corrected every thing of this kind according to his best judgment, and as it might have been presumed the Author would have done, if he had been spared to a longer life. But as it has been observed, the Editor's attention being called off to pursuits of another nature, he was obliged to relax in that design, and in consulting one of Mr. GODFREY's friends, on whose judgment he always had the strongest reliance, it occasioned, in some places, his remitting this intention. The reasons that prevailed on him are contained in the following Letter; and if it proves as satisfactory to the reader, as it was to him, there will be no further apology wanted for the present form in which these Juvenile Pieces, of our much lamented Author, appear.

SIR,

IT is greatly to your credit, that the warm friendship, which subsisted between the late Mr. GODFREY and you, is affectionately extended to his memory, and has induced you to undertake the labour of collecting his Posthumous Pieces to be publish'd in one volume, with those more corrected and finished Performances, which made their appearance in his life-time, after passing thro' the hands of some of his friends, whose judgment he esteemed You tell me, you have been inform'd, that the Authors of the Monthly Review, in England, have not given a very high character of the "COURT OF FANCY," which we had considered as one of Mr. GODFREY's capital performances; and you ask whether it might not be proper to make such corrections in his posthumous Works, especially the "Prince of Parthia," as the Author himself, if now alive, would thankfully accept from his friends; particularly in regard to his Pointing, and the Accentuation of some of his words and classical names?

As to what is said in the *Review*, it would not displease you, if you had seen it. The judgment given of Mr. Godfrey's *poetical abilities*, by the Authors of that work, who had seen only a few of his performances, does not differ much from that of his warmest and most indulgent friends, who have seen the whole. "Mr. Godfrey "(say the Authors) possesses a considerable degree of poetical imagination, but little "learning, as appears from his improper accentuation of classical names." They mention the Pieces in the American Magazine, which first procured him his poetical reputation; and add that "they remember, to have since

"..... the P...... (.......... Piece call'd "VICTORY") on the fuc-
" .... the Britifh Americ in America." "He certainly h s a genius; and we are forry
" we had no redrainat to the profeffion." "This is their conclufion, and the fubftance
of what they fay; in which Mr. Charles Jenkins will join with them. But as want
of leisure was his misfortune, not his fault, the noble efforts of his natural genius
deferve the greater praife; and this the Reviewers confefs by faying "They wifh
" well to learning in the Colonies, and would not difcourage any efforts that way,
" by the rigour of criticifm." -

'Tis kind not to difcourage, but it is ftill more kind pofitively to encourage; and
it were to be wifh'd that the Reviewers had found room to give fome examples of
our Author's ftrong imagination and picturefque genius from the "Court of Fancy."
The following might have been chofen among many others. After defcribing the
Temple of Fancy, he gives this grand defcription of the Goddefs Fancy herfelf.

" High in the midft, rais'd on her rolling throne,
" Sublimely eminent, bright Fancy fhone, &c.
" A radiant bough, enfign of her command,
" Of polifh'd gold, wav'd in her lily hand —
" In filver traces, fix'd unto her car
" Four fnowy Swans, proud of th' imperial Fair,
" Wing'd lightly on : each, in gay beauty drefs,
" Smooth'd the foft plumage that adorn'd her breaft;
" Sacred to her the lucent chariot drew —
" Or whither wildly thro' the air fhe flew,
" Or whither to the dreary fhades of night,
" Opprefs'd with gloom, fhe downwards bends her flight, -
" Or proud afpiring, fought the bleft abodes,
" And boldly fhot among th' aftonifh'd Gods." —

I need not hint to you the propriety of all this Painting "Fancy mounted fublimely on a rolling throne" - "fnowy Swans" whirling her car, with winged fpeed,
whitherfoever fhe pleafes ; in which our Author was no doubt animated by thofe beautiful lines of Shakefpeare, in the motto to his performance ——

" The Poet's eye, in a fine frenzy rolling,
" Doth glance from Heaven to Earth, from Earth to Heaven!"

I have, for brevity, omitted feveral lines in our Author's defcription of Fancy herfelf;
but the following lines, where he makes the Mufes Graces and Loves, with their
true offspring, Poetry, Painting and Mufic, to be the attendants on Fancy, in the
characters of the three great ancient mafters, Homer, Apelles, and Timotheus — thefe
lines, I fay, are conceived with fuch claffical propriety, and exprefs'd with fuch laconic
elegance, that they well deferve notice.

" On

" On her right hand, appear'd the joyful *Nine*,
" And on her left, the *Graces* all-divine ;
" Young infant-*Love*, foft, on her breaft reclin'd,
" And with his Mother's glowing beauty fhin'd.
" Her fav'rite Sons were rang'd in order round,
" In three bright bands, with deathlefs laurel crown'd ;
" Great *Homer*, here enjoy'd fuperior day,
" Illuminated by bright Fancy's ray ;
" *Apelles*, there, whofe magic hand could give
" Form to the mafs, and bid the *Fiction* live ;
" *Timotheus* next, whofe animated lyre,
" Cold Grief could charm, and thoughtlefs Rage infpire."—

POPE himfelf would not have thought the beft of his writings difhonor'd by fuch nervous, well-imagin'd and harmonious lines as thefe. Nor is the humble place, which our Author has given himfelf, among the attendants of *Fancy*, lefs to be admir'd for the modefty and delicate beauty of the thought —

" Clofe at her FEET, a Bard, in raptures loft,
" Was plac'd, and wildly round his eye-balls toft —
" Great *Fancy* was his theme ! the foothing ftrain,
" In floods of pleafure, thrill'd thro' every vein—

His addrefs to *Fancy* is very beautiful, and alfo his following apology for intruding into her court—

" With lowly reverence I hither came,
" Not to deride, but to adore thy name ;
" To thee I ever dedicate my fong,
" And hail thy glories, 'midft this fuppliant throng—

He then reprefents the Goddefs as indulgent to his prayer, in the following rap-turous lines —

——" Here, mortal ! take this lyre,
" Strike bold the ftrings, and fing as I infpire.
" Humbly I bow'd, her mild commands obey'd,
" And carelefs o'er the lyre my fingers laid ;
" And foon, with wild poetic rage poffefs'd,
" All my frame fhook, and lab'ring heav'd my breaft.

His chufing " Zephyr" as the meffenger of *Fancy*, and his various defcriptions on this head, could arife only from true poetic genius. His Account of the Ægyptian *fuperftitions*, the Heathen worfhip, &c. fhews great reading in the ancient mythology

and

and history, as well as an attentive perusal of the translations of Greek and Roman classics; and what more could be expected from a youth that was only acquainted with the English, and a little of the French tongue?

    " Toward the rosy East, great *Mythra* shone,
    " Bright in the glories of a rising Sun.
    " Beneath in solemn pomp, with hands uprear'd
    " In flowing robes the *Magi* all appear'd — &c.
     " Northward fierce †*Woden* stood, with terrors crown'd,
    " And angry †*Thor* threw heedless thunder round—
    " Old *Merlin* struck the lyre, the wond'ring throng
    " Attend around to his prophetic song —
    " Southward, disorder'd figures struck my eyes,
    " *Monkies* and *Serpents* rais'd to Deities,— &c.
    " Maim'd *Memnon* there seem'd on his ‡harp to play,
    " And hail *Osiris* bringing on the day.
    " Pale *Isis* cre'cent faintly glimmer'd here,
    " And barking ‖*Anubis* display'd the Year—&c."

Our Author's succeeding descriptions of Poetry, Painting, Sculpture, Architecture, Astronomy, Philosophy, &c. are equally pleasing—a few of the lines will shew this.

    " *Astronomy*, with proud aspiring eye,
    " Gaz'd on the glowing beauties of the sky.
    " Her vest with glittering stars was spangled o'er,
    " And in her hand a telescope she bore.
    " With this she mark'd the rolling planes way,
    " Or where portentous comets dreadful stray —
    " Tho' last not least, *Philosophy* was seen,
    " Slow was her step, and awful was her mien.
    " A volume open, in her hand she held,
    " With Nature's law the ample page was fill'd.
    " 'Tis her's great Nature's wond'rous Depths t' explore,
    " Or to the Gods in heavenly rap'ure soar —
    " Fair Truth she led, in spotless white array'd,
    " And pleasing Beauty, sweet celestial maid.
    " Where *Truth* and *Nature* aid the great design,
    " BEAUTY attends and makes it all divine." —

---

† Gods of the Northern Nations.

‡ Alluding to the story of *Memnon*'s statue in the temple of Serapis, at Thebes, fabulously said to send harmonious founds from its mouth, when first touch'd by the rays of the rising fun.

‖ An Egyptian idol, with a dog's head.—*Latratorem, Semicanem Deum*—saith Virg. Æn. 8.

From the *Court* of *Fancy* he makes a fudden tranfition to the *Court* of *Delufion,*—where —

> ——" Within confin'd
> " Gay Fictions lurk, and Dreams of every kind —
> " Dreft by her hand, they fhine with mimic bloom,
> " Or, at her word, their *Nothingnefs* refume."—

The word " Nothingnefs" is peculiarly expreffive in this line. Under this head, the airy fchemes of Ambition, thirft of Power, Superftition, Jealoufy, Avarice, falfe Honour, falfe Affectation of Learning, &c. are defcribed—I fhall only quote a few lines, out of feveral pages.

> " Others, more bold, majeftic 'portments take,
> " And plague, delighted, thofe who dream awake.
> " Such are the dreams of thofe who thirft for power,
> " The fuperftitious, and a thoufand more.
> " Others ufurp the features of the dead,
> " And fhake the torch around the murd'rer's bed ;
> " Affright the vigil, or in wanton mirth, ·
> " Make fools feek hidden treafure in the earth,"—

Our *Virtuofo* and butter-fly men are well ridicul'd in what follows—

> " The next to her approach'd a reverend dame,
> " In trophies *great,* from *Infects* torn, fhe came.
> " With ftately ftep fhe trod the plain along,
> " And threw her treafure 'mid th' admiring throng.
> " Forward, with joy, each curious mortal fprang,
> " This caught a gaudy wing, and that a pointed fang."

The *Moral* of his conclufion is excellent—

> " As thus I onward mov'd with wand'ring pace,
> " And view'd the varied wonders of the place ;
> " Juft Heaven, I cry'd, Oh ! give me to reftrain,
> " *Imagination* with a fteady rein !
> " Tho' oft fhe leads thro' *Pleafure's* flowery ways,
> " In *Error's* thorny path fhe fometimes ftrays.
> " Let me my hours with folid *Judgment* fpend,
> " Nor to *Delufion's* airy dreams attend ;
> " By REASON guided, we fhall only know
> " Thofe heavenly joys which FANCY can beftow."

Thus you fee I have not altered my judgment of this Poem. There is a proper

c   poetical

poetical spirit supported thro' the whole; and but few places where I think it could be amended. Many beautiful passages might be selected from his other Pieces; such as the Character of General *Wolfe*, Pastoral 3. The *Garden-Description* in the *Assembly* of *Birds*, &c. ———

I come now to the question you ask,—" Whether it might not be proper to make " such corrections in Mr. Godfrey's posthumous Pieces, as he himself, if alive, " would thankfully accept from his friends?"

In answer to this I would observe, that such corrections and alterations as were made in Mr. Godfrey's Pieces in his life-time, upon hints from his friends, and with the approbation of his own judgment, were thereby rendered his own. Sometimes he would insert such corrections, as they were offered to him; and othertimes substitute something in their stead, better than his own first thoughts, or the amendments propos'd by his friends. It was in this last method, by improving on the criticisms, and remarks of every judicious friend, that the writings of Pope and some of our greatest Poets, appeared so elegantly nervous and correct.

No doubt, sundry corrections are wanted in some of Mr. Godfrey's posthumous Pieces, and especially in the Prince of *Parthia*; I will mention a few. In Pastoral 1st, tho' he has sometimes accented the word " *Alexis* " right, and seems to have known the proper pronunciation of it—yet in the following couplet which occurs thrice, he has occasionally placed the accent wrong—

" Droop, droop ye groves; ye plains, in silence mourn,
" Let nought be gay, 'til *Alexis* return—

It might be amended various ways—

Droop, droop ye groves, and all ye plains be dumb,
Let nought be joyful 'til *Alexis* come.—

Or preserving the first rhime, and leaving out the name *Alexis*, which is not material, being in the couplet immediately preceeding—

Droop, droop ye groves, ye fields, in silence mourn,
Let nought be joyful till the Swain's return.

Or preserving the name—

Alexis gone! be dumb, each grove and plain,
Let nought be joyful, 'till I see my Swain.

So in the same Pastoral, the word " lay " is not English, but the couplet may be amended with the smallest alteration—

" Here by my side, my pipe shall useless *lay*,
" Unheeded now Alexis is away."—

To

To be corrected thus:

Here by my fide, my pipe fhall ufelefs lie,
Unheeded now Alexis is not nigh.

In this couplet, it is to be obferved, that Mr. Godfrey places the accent on Alexis right.

In Paftoral 2d, are thefe lines—

" Witnefs, ye groves, and *eke*, ye powers divine,
" How oft *fhe's* fworn her faithlefs heart was mine.
" Now, fir'd by female pride, fhe fcorns the truth,
" And gives to wealthy *Ageon* her youth.
" He's rich in num'rous flocks, fcarce knows his ftore,
" My love is all, nor can I boaft of more."

What is faulty in thefe lines, proceeds from unneceffary elifions, the obfolete word "eke" and the fpelling the claffical name wrong; for I do not at prefent remember any fuch name as *Ageon*, and if there be fuch a one, it is here wrong accented. The fmalleft alteration amends the whole;

Witnefs ye groves, and all ye powers divine,
How oft fhe fwore her faithlefs heart was mine.
Now, fir'd by female pride, fhe fcorns the truth,
And to the rich *Ægæon* gives her youth.
Of numerous flocks the fwain fcarce knows his ftore,
My love is all, nor can I boaft of more.

A few lines afterwards he places the accent differently on the fame word " Ageon;" which fhews that, in his firft hafty draughts, he did not even ftay fo far to attend to thefe leffer mattes, as to make one part confiftent with another.

There is the fame fault in placing the name " Amphion" a few ftanzas below, which a fmall tranfpofition amends.

As to the *Tragedy*, it is evidently very unfinifhed, efpecially in the laft act; and nothing but that fondnefs which every Author has for a performance when it comes firft from his pen, would have made him propofe it for the ftage. But as he knew the Company was about to break up, and he might not foon have another opportunity of trying his fuccefs this way, he was willing to offer it; and as the prefent elifions and unfinifhed lines, would not have been perceived from the mouth of the Actors, he would have had leifure before the publication to correct every thing which he might have found faulty, in the diction and meafure. As to the fentiments, they are generally noble, and worthy of the fubject; and in refpect to the plan, it would not be juft to enquire whether the *Unities* of the *Drama* be all rigidly obferved by a youth,

who,

who, perhaps, never heard of the rules of *Horace*, or the *Stagyrite*; yet our Author's own peculiar Genius, and ideas of Propriety, have help'd him furprizingly out, in this matter.

The fame overfights which I have taken notice of in fome of the Paftorals, like-wife occur in this Tragedy.

" What pleafure, *Phraates*, muft fwell his bofom,
" To fee the proftrate nation all around him,
" And know *he's* made them happy! to hear them
" Teafe the Gods to fhower their bleffings on him?"

For which, might be read as follows ——

What joy, *Phraates*, muft expand his bofom,
To fee the proftrate nation all around him,
Made happy by his virtues! and to hear them
Weary the Gods to fhow'r their bleffings on him?

In the two firft of the three following lines, there are bad grammar, and bad accentuation.

" While fhame and rout *difperfes* all her fons,
" Barzaphernes purfues the fugitives,
The few whom fav'ring night redeem'd from flaughter."

They might be alter'd thus—

While fhame and rout difperfe her haplefs fons;
Bold Barzaphernes feeks, with vengeful arm,
The few whom fav'ring night redeem'd from flaughter.

A little lower we have thefe lines—

" Arfaces heard,
" And thro' the fwelling waves he rufh'd to fave
" His drowning brother, and gave him life;
" And for the boon the ingrate pays him hate."—

where the 3d line wants a fyllable, and there is a difagreeable jingle in the others. They might run thus—

——Arfaces heard,
And rufhing, inftant, thro' th' oppofing tide,
To fave his finking brother, gave him life,
Who for the boon ignobly pays him hate.

I could eafily fend you more examples of corrections that might be made in this and Mr. Godfrey's other Pofthumous Pieces, which you put into my hands; but I am fully perfuaded that it will be fafer for you, and perhaps more acceptable to many readers, to lay thefe remains of Mr. Godfrey before the Public, in their genuine original ftate, than venture on any material alterations, which might not after all be alike agreeable to every body; and perhaps in fome cafes be for the worfe. For inftance, in the following line—

    " Still in intricate mazes round I run"—

the accent on the word "intricate" is wrong; and a perfon defirous to place it right and make the line fmooth, would correct it thus——

    In mazes intricate ftill round I run—

But I could not advife fuch an alteration as this; for it may probably have been the Author's intention in this line to make the found an echo to the fenfe; and if fo, the Intricacy of the line, and difficulty of the pronunciation, with the two *in*'s joined together, are fufficiently expreffive of the fubject.

To offer fmaller corrections of this kind, might be the work of any hand; but to reach the heights to which our Poet has arrived in many parts of his writings, and of this Tragedy itfelf, is the lot of but a few.

How ftrongly is the following curfe exprefs'd!

    " O may he never know a father's fondnefs,
    " Or know it to his forrow! may his hopes
    " Of joy be cut like mine, and his fhort life
    " Be one continued tempeft—if he lives,
    " Let him be curft with jealoufy and fear—
    " May tort'ring Hope prefent the flowing cup,
    " Then, hafty, fnatch it from his eager thirft,
    " And when he dies, bafe treachery be the means."

As a contraft to the *fierce paffions* in the preceeding lines, may be quoted the following humane fentiments.

    " O 'tis a heavenly virtue, when the heart
    " Can feel the forrows of another's bofom!
    " It dignifies the man. The ftupid wretch
    " Who knows not this fenfation, is an image,
    " And wants the feeling to make up a life."

I fhall add but one quotation more from this Tragedy——

    " How fhall I thank you, ye bright glorious Beings!
    " Shall I in humble adoration bow,
    " Or fill the earth with your refounding praife?

                                         " No

" No, this I leave to noify hypocrites—
" A mortal's tongue difgraces fuch a theme.
" But heaven delights where filent gratitude
" Mounts each afpiring thought to its bright throne,
" Nor leaves to language aught: words may indeed
" From man to man their feveral wants exprefs,
" Heaven afks the purer incenfe of the heart."

Upon the whole, I perfuade my felf that, the fevereft critic, looking over fmaller matters, will allow thefe writings of Mr. Godfrey, to be aptly characteriz'd, in the following lines from the Court of Fancy—

" Bold Fancy's hand th' amazing pile uprears,
" In every part ftupendous fkill appears ;
" In beautiful diforder, yet compleat,
" The ftructure fhines irregularly great."

I am, Sir,

Yours, &c.

SUBSCRIBERS NAMES.

A

Hon. WILLIAM ALLEN, Efq, Chief Juftice, of this Province.
Reverend Francis Alifon, D. D. Vice-Provoft of the College and Academy of Philadelphia.
John Allen, Efq;
Andrew Allen, Efq;
James Allen, Efq;
Revd. Mr. John George Alfentz.
William Atlee, Efq; Lancafter.
Capt. Samuel Atlee, Pequea.
Mr Benjamin Auftin.
Dr. Ralph Afhton.
Mr. John Andrews. } Tutors in the C.
  Alexander Alexander. } A. Philadelphia.
Affociation Library Company of Philadelphia.
Mr. Ifaac Allman.
Capt. John Afhmead.

B

Hon. Col. *Henry Bouquet.*
Capt. James Blair.
Mr. *Thomas Barclay.*
  John Bell.
Daniel Benezet, Efq;
Dr. Phineas Bond.
Mr. Thomas Bond, jun.
Alexander Barclay, Efq;
Mifs Elizabeth Bond.
Revd. Thomas Barton, A. M. ⎤
  Miffionary, 4.   ⎟
James Burd, ⎤ Efqrs.   ⎬ Lancafter.
John Barr, ⎦   ⎟
Doctor Boyd.   ⎦
Mr. John Baynton, 2.
  Samuel Burge.
  Philip Benezet.
  Roger Bowman.
  William Bartram, jun.⎤
  James Bailey.   ⎬ North Carolina.
  Abraham Bickley, 2. ⎦
  Clement Biddle.
  Gunning Bedford.
  Jofeph Burn.
  John Barns.

Jofeph Burt, Student, ⎤ of Jerfey
Benjamin Brearly, Student, ⎬ College.
Jonathan Baldwin, A. M. ⎦
Mr. Andrew Boyd.
  Philip Bufh.
  Thomas Bradford.
John Beveridge, A. M. Profeffor of Languages in the College and Academy of Philadelphia.
Mr. Ignatius Baker. ⎤ Students in the fame.
  Samuel Benezet. ⎦

C

Benjamin Chew, Efq; Attorney General.
Hon. William Coleman, Efq;
Mr. William Campbell.
  Alexander Chapman. ⎬ North Carolina.
  Robert Cohren. ⎦
Mrs. Eleanor Campbell, Lancafter.
Mr. William Cliffton.
  Matthew Clarkfon.
  Samuel Cheefman.
  Charles Cox.
  Archibald M'Call.
Dr. Gerardus Clarkfon.
Mrs. Mary Cotringer.
Mr. John Chevalier.
  Peter Chevalier, jun.
  Philip Cole.
  Thomas Coombe, Student in the College of Philadelphia.
  Abraham Cannel, Maryland.
  John Child.
  William Carter.
  Samuel Carfon.
  James Carter.
  Julius Clare, 2.
  James Cruickfhank.
  George Corbin.
  Jofeph Chambers.
  James Claypool.
  Lambert Cadwalader.
  Curtis Clay.

D

Revd. Jacob Duché, A. M. one of the Affiftant Minifters of Chrift Church and St. Peter's, 2.

Mr,

Mr. Benjamin Davies, Merchant, 3.
John Dorfius.
William Davis, ⎫ Efqrs. ⎫ North Caro-
Alexander Duncan, ⎭ ⎭ lina.
Mr. Walter Duroie.
Jofephus Dariel, Bermuda.
James Dickinfon.
Benjamin Duffield.
Jofias Davis.
Philemon Dickinfon.
John Duffield
Charles Dilworth.
Jofiah Franklin Davenport.
Doctor Duffiel.
Mr. John De-normadie.

E

Mr. Samuel Eldridge, 6.
Hudfon Emlen, 2.
George Emlen.

F

Benjamin Franklin, Efq; L. L. D. F. R. S. 12.
His Excellency William Franklin, Efq; Go-
vernor of New-Jerfey.
Col. Turbut Francis.
Mr. Caleb Foulke.
Amos Foulke.
Moore Furman, 2.
Samuel Foulke.
David Franks.
Henry Collins Flagg, Rhode-Ifland.
William Forfter, A. B. Jerfey College.

G

Dr. George Glentworth, 2.
Col. Caleb Grainger, North Carolina.
Mr. William Greenway.
John Green.
John Gibfon.
Mifs Elizabeth Garregues.
Mr. William Gallagher.
Jofeph Galloway, Efq;
Mr. Thomas Guy.
Germantown Library Company.

H

Richard Hockley, Efq;
Benjamin Heron, Efq;
Provincial Secretary. ⎫ North-Carolina.
Cornelius Harnett, Efq; ⎬
Mr. Obadiah Holt. ⎭
Daniel Hughes.

Francis Hopkinfon, Efq;
Mr. William Hopkins.
William Hamilton.
Ifaac Hunt. 2.
Samuel Haffel, 2.
Levi Hollingfworth, 6.
John Hart.
Nathaniel Hazard, A. B. ⎫
Mr. Richard Hufon. ⎬ ⎫ Students ⎫ Jerfey College.
Jofeph Hafbrouck. ⎭ ⎬
Jacob Hafbrouck. ⎭
David Howell. ⎭
Alexander Hanfon, Student in the Col-
lege of Philadelphia.
Mr. Robert Harding.
James Humphreys.
John William Hoffman.
Adam Hubley, 2.
Samuel Hudfon.

I

Mr. Abel James, 2.
Revd. Mr. Charles Inglis, Miffionary at Dover.
Mr. Jonathan Jones.
Robert Johnfon, North-Carolina.
John Jones, jun.
Mrs. Rebecca Jennings, Bermuda.
Mr. Reuben Jarman.
Mr. Jeffe Jacobs.
Jofeph Jacobs.
Robert Strettel Jones.
Juliana Library Company of Lancafter.

K

Revd. Ebenezer Kinnerfley, A. M. Profeffor
of Englifh and Oratory, in the College of
Philadelphia.
Dr. John Kearfley, jun. 2.
Mr. Philip Kearney.
John Kelly.
Jofeph Kirk.
Henry Keppele, jun.
Jofeph Kendall.

L

John Lawrence, ⎫ Efqrs
Thomas Lawrence, ⎭
Mr. William Lackly.
Alexander Lunnan.
John Long, Lancafter.
Capt. Hugh Lidlie, Connecticut, 2.
Mr. John Langdale, jun. 2.

Mr.

Mr. John Lucken, Surveyor-General.
John Lucken. ·
Joseph Lancaster.
Nathaniel Lewis.

M

Samuel Mifflin, Esq;
William Moore, Esq;
John Moore. Esq;
Mr. John Malcolm.
William Masters.
John Maxfield.
Mrs. Anne Morgan.
Miss Elizabeth Morgan.
Mr. Robert Morris.
Col. James Moore.   ⎫
Archibald Mc. Clane, Esq; ⎬ North-Carolina·
Mr. Archibald M' Duffei.   ⎪
Alexander Martin.   ⎭
Robert Moore.
Dr. Charles Moore.
Revd. Mr. Murray, Missionary at Reading.
Mr. Samuel Miles.
Miss Nancy Mordgarige.
Mr. Archibald Milroy.
John Morris, jun. Esq;
Mr. Henry Mitchell.
Matthew Mease.
John Mears.
Jonathan Morris.
John-Murgatride.
George Morgan.
Cadwallader Morris.
William Morris.
Henry Miller, 12.

N

Charles Norris. Esq;
Mr. John Nixon, 2.
Mrs. Anne Nitsfield, North Carolina.

O

Mr. John Ord.

P

Honourable J O H N P E N N, Esq; Go-
vernour of this Province. &c.
Revd. Richard Peters, Rector of the united
Churches of Christ Church and St. Peter's.
William Peters, Esq;
Richard Peters. jun. A. B.
William Plumsted. Esq; 2.
William Purviance, Esq; North Carolina.

Mr. Edward Pennington.
Samuel Pleasents.-
James Peters, Druggist, Lancaster.
Joseph Paschall.
Joseph Pennel.
Jonathan Potts.
Thomas Pratt.
Joseph Pemberton, 2.
Caleb Parry.
Samuel Purviance.
John Porters, A. B.
Mr. Charles Pettit.
Ebenezer Pemberton, Student. ⎫ Jersey
Joseph Periam, A. B.   ⎬ College.

R

Septimus Robeson, Esq;
Mr. Barnet Richards.
William Richards.
Robert Ritchie.
William Ritchie.
John Robeson, North Carolina.
Edward Robeson.
James Ralfe, ⎫
George Ross, ⎬ Esqrs. Lancaster.
Joseph Rose, ⎭
Mr. Alexander Robinson, 2.
James Read,   ⎫ Esqrs. Reading.
Thomas Rutter, ⎭
Mr. William Rawlings, 2.
Theodorick Romains, ⎫ Stu- ⎫ Jersey
David Ramsay,   ⎬ dents. ⎬ College.
Topping Reeve, A. B.   ⎭
Benjamin Rush, A. M.
Mr. John Reily, Conveyancer.
Cæsar Roach, Esq; Antigua.

S

Reverend William Smith, D. D. Provost of
the College and Academy of Philadel-
phia, 4.
Hon. Alexander Stedman, Esq;
Mr. Charles Stedman.
Joseph Shippen, jun. Esq; Provincial Secretary.
William Shippen, jun. M. D.
Mr. Samuel Harriet Solavan.
William Smith.
Capt. Alexander Sage.
Mr. Robert Shaw   ⎫
Patrick Stewart. ⎬ North-Carolina.
James Stewart.   ⎭

d

Miſs Elizabeth Stedman.
Edward Shippen Eſq; Prothonotary. } Lan-
Mr. Francis Sanderſon. } caſter.
John Stone. }
Thomas Smith. Eſq; Bermuda.
Miſs Elizabeth Syng.
Mr. Robert Shewell.
    Samuel Sanſom, jun. 2.
    James Searle.
    Simon Sparkland.
    Iſaac Stillman, } Students. } Jerſey
    Benjamin Steele, } } College.
David Smith, A. M.
Jonathan Smith, A. M. 2.
Mr. William Smith.
    Joſeph Saunders.
Dr. Benjamin Stakes.
Mr. Walter Shee.
    David Sample, Student, in the College of
    Philadelphia.
Amos Strettle, Eſq;
Mr. Alexander Stuart.
    Samuel Shaw.
    Lodowick Sprogell.
    John Sprogell, jun.
        T
Revd. Mr. William Thompſon, Miſſionary,
    for Cumberland County.
Joſeph Turner, Eſq;
Dr. Maluchi Treat.

Thomas Tredwell, A. B. } Jerſey Col-
James Thompſon, A. B. Tutor, } lege.
Mr. David Thomas.
    Samuel Taylor, 6.
    Joſeph Thomas.
    Samuel Treat.
        U
Union Library Company of Philadelphia.
        W
Mr. Samuel Wharton, 2.
    Joſeph Wharton, 2.
    Daniel Wiſter 2.
Capt. Iſaac Laſcelles Winn, 2.
Capt. George Chriſtopher Winn.
Mr. Stephen Watts.
    John White.
    Alexander Wilcocks.
    William White, Student in the College
    of Philadelphia.
    Charles Wharton.
    Samuel Wheeler.
    William Watkins, North Carolina.
    Hugh Wilſon, Lancaſter.
    Nicholas Way.
    William Warner.
    William Wood.
    George Weſcott.
    John Wood.
        Y
Mr. James Young. 2.

The CONTENTS.

E R R A T A.

IN the Preface, Page 7, Line 1, for *consicious*, read *conspicuous*. In the Poems, p. 19, l. 2. for *lightn'd*, r. *lighten'd*. p. 25, l. 17, for *wonted*, r. *wanted*. p. 26, l. 5, for *sadn'd*, r. *sadned*. p. 36, l. 4, for *Zephyr's*, r. *Zephyrs*. p. 50, l. 10. for *Phæton*, r. *Phaeton*. p. 54, l. 11, for *rev'rence*, r. *reverence*. p. 97, l. 10. for *saf'ty*, r. *safety*. p. 101, l. 12, for, *Tisaphernes*, r. *Tissaphernes*. p. 119, l. 21. for, *infamcy*, r. *infamy*. p. 131, l. 9, for, *set*, r. *fit*. p. 192, l. 3, for *'ll*, r. *I'll*.

Page 19 line 6th for exspires, read expires

For the above errata, instead of p. 101 line 12 read

p. 101 line 9. Page 98, line 11 for falchin

read falchion.

E L E G Y,

To the Memory of Mr THOMAS GODFREY.

Quis defiderio fit pudor aut modus
Tam chari capitis?　　　　　HOR.

WHERE nodding yews the folemn grove imbrown,
Where ivy creeps, and gloomy cyprefs frown,
While low'ring clouds the face of Phæbe fhade,
And fleeting ghofts glide filent o'er the glade,
There let me lie——by lighter ills unmov'd,
And weep the mem'ry of the Youth I lov'd.
Melpomene, whofe plaintive harp ne'er knew,
Aught but heart-piercing founds of fadeft woe,
With mournful voice, and ever-melting tongue,
Join in my grief, and aid th' elegiac fong.

Death's icy hand has clos'd my Damon's eyes,
His corfe entomb'd, in fleep eternal lies.
Cold is that breaft which ev'ry virtue fir'd,
(Where mufic dwelt), and all the Nine infpir'd.

Silent,

Silent, no more the tuneful tongue shall charm,
No more with glow benign the cheek shall warm;
The death-fixt eye no more with lustre beam,
No more the placid brow shall smile serene.
And, ah! that heart the seat of truth before,
With friendship's sacred fires shall beat no more:
Black-rob'd oblivion's baleful wing outspread,
Shrouds his lov'd form, and ev'ry charm is fled.
His sable reign the tyrant whelms o'er-all,
Thus the proud perish, thus the virtuous fall!
As silver streams in easy mazes glide,
And to the main in tribute roll their tide,
Or bursting flames in curling volumes rise
Seeking their place congenial in the skies;
Thus Man is born, thus haste his fleeting days,
Transient his glory as the Meteor's blaze.
Nature's great law stern death impartial sounds,
Hurls the barb'd dart and undistinguish'd wounds:
The regal sceptre in the dust he throws,
Rends the plum'd helmet from the Hero's brows,
And tears from beauty's cheek the blooming rose;
Strikes manly vigor with'ring, in life's prime,
Bids palsied age its trembling breath resign,
Tears from the bleeding breast the infant heir,
In vain the parent-sigh, in vain the melting pray'r:
The friend belov'd——Oh! burst my beating heart,
Here the dread tyrant quenches ev'ry dart!

On

On thee, dear Youth, the blow was foft impreft,
Ages of blifs fucceed and golden reft;
'Tis mine alone to drain th' envenom'd bowl,
The fhaft fuftain that rankles in the foul;
Sighing to recollect each joyous day,
That friendfhip's Cherub fmile made ever gay;
In life's firft dawn, with infant paffion fir'd,
One path entic'd us, and one wifh infpir'd;
By friendfhip warm'd (tho' ftrangers to the name,
'Til love of fifter-arts encreas'd the flame);
On the foft mufic of thy lyre I hung,
Charm'd with the early lay fo fweetly fung,
I hail'd! with rapture thy afcending fame!
And faw from ripen'd years, a deathlefs name!
In vain I figh!—the fun-clad vifion 's o'er,
Thofe ftrains by heav'n infpir'd fhall charm no more!

Dear fhade, farewell!——it fmiling quits its clay
Waves the glad hand, and mounts the dazzling way.
See! glitt'ring bands in angel tranfport join!
Waft him to endlefs blifs with fongs divine!
Hark! how the founds feraphic ftrike the ear!
O virtue! now thy raptures are fincere!

Ye gentle Swains of *Carolina's* fhore,
Who knew my Damon, (now, alas! no more),
By moon-light round his hallow'd grave repair,
Strew fweeteft flow'rs, and drop a forrowing tear;

With

With never-fading laurel ſhade his tomb,
And bid the riſing bay for ever bloom,
Teach ſpringing flow'rs their purpl'd heads to riſe,
And ſweetly twining, write, *Here Virtue lies*.
Sing in ſad ſtrains each venerable name,
In Fortune's ſpite, that ſtruggl'd up to fame;
By Virtue led life's rugged road along,
Their lives inſtructive as their ſweeteſt ſong.
Say, while their praiſes tremble on the tongue,
Thus liv'd this youthful Bard, thus gentle Damon ſung.

What tho', ah! much-lov'd Youth 'mong ſtrangers thrown
Thy relicks ſleep, beneath a nameleſs ſtone,
No ſculptur'd glories o'er thy aſhes plac'd,
That weeping ſeem to ſpeak what once thou waſt;
What, tho' no tuneful Bard thy praiſes ſings,
And only friendſhip ſounds the jarring ſtrings;
Yet, with the good and juſt, thy name ſhall live,
'Tis Virtue's ſacred right—this pageant pomp can't give.

J. GREEN.

ELEGY,

To the Memory of the fame.

O Death! thou victor of the human frame!
The foul's poor fabrick trembles at thy name!
How long fhall man be urg'd to dread thy fway
For thofe whom thou untimely tak'ft away?
Life's blooming fpring juft opens to our eyes,
And ftrikes the fenfes with a fweet furprize,
When thy fierce arm uplifts the fatal blow
That hurls us breathlefs to the earth below.

Sudden as darts the lightning thro' the fky
Around the globe thy various weapons fly:
Here war's red engines heap the field with flain,
And pallid ficknefs there extends thy reign;
Here the foft Virgin weeps her Lover dead,
There Maiden beauty finks the graceful head,
Here Infants grieve their Parents are no more,
There rev'rent Sires their Childrens deaths deplore.
Here the fad friend—O! fave the facred name,
Yields half his foul to thy relentlefs claim;
O pardon, pardon the defcending tear!
Friendfhip commands, and not the Mufes here.
O fay, thou much lov'd dear departed fhade,
To what celeftial region haft thou ftray'd?

Where

Where is that vein of thought, that noble fire
Which fed thy foul, and bade the world admire?
That manly ſtrife with fortune to be juſt,
That love of praiſe? an honourable thirſt!
The Soul, alas! has fled to endleſs day,
And left its houſe a mould'ring maſs of clay.

There, where no fears invade, nor ills moleſt,
Thy foul ſhall dwell immortal with the bleſt;
In that bright realm, where deareſt friends no more
Shall from each other's throbbing breaſts be tore,
Where all thoſe glorious ſpirits ſit enſhrin'd,
The juſt, the good, the virtuous of mankind.
There ſhall fair angels in a radiant ring,
And the great SON of Heav'ns eternal KING,
Proclaim thee welcome to the bliſsful ſkies,
And wipe the tears for ever from thy eyes.

How did we hope—alas! the hope how vain!
To hear thy future more enripen'd ſtrain;
When fancy's fire with judgement had combin'd
To guide each effort of th' enraptur'd mind.
Yet are thoſe youthful glowing lays of thine
The emanations of a ſoul divine;
Who heard thee ſing but felt ſweet muſic's dart
In thrilling tranſports pierce his captiv'd heart?
Whether ſoft melting airs attun'd thy ſong,
Or pleas'd to pour the thundring verſe along,

Still

Still nobly great, true offspring of the Nine,
Alas! how blafted in thy glorious prime!
So when firft opes the eye-lids of the morn,
A radiant purple does the heav'ns adorn,
Frefh fmiling glory ftreaks the fkies around,
And gaily filvers each enamel'd mound,
'Til fome black ftorm o'erclouds the æther fair,
And all its beauties vanifh into air.

Sranger, who e'er thou art, by fortune's hand
Toft on the baleful *Carolinian* ftrand,
Oh! if thou feeft perchance the Poet's grave
The facred fpot with tears of forrow lave;
Oh! fhade it, fhade it with ne'er fading bays.
Hallow'd 's the place where gentle Godfrey lays.
(So may no fudden dart from death's dread bow
Far from the friends thou lov'ft e'er lay thee low),
There may the weeping morn its tribute bring,
And angels fhield it with their golden wing,
'Til the laft trump fhall burft the womb of night,
And the purg'd atoms to their Soul unite!

October 1, 1763.   N. EVANS.

JUVENILE

JUVENILE POEMS,

ON

VARIOUS SUBJECTS.

B

JUVENILE POEMS, &c.

THE INVITATION. 1758.

DAMON.

HASTE! SYLVIA! hafte, my charming Maid!
 Let's leave thefe fafhionable toys;
 Let's feek the fhelter of fome fhade,
And revel in ne'er fading joys.
See fpring in liv'ry gay appears,
 And winter's chilly blafts are fled;
Each grove its leafy honours rears,
 And meads their lovely verdure fpraad!

SYLVIA.

Yes Damon, glad I'll quit the town,
 Its gaities now languid feem;
Then fweets to luxury unknown
 We'll tafte, and fip th' untainted ftream.
In Summer's fultry noon-tide heat,
 I'll lead thee to the fhady grove;
There hufh thy cares, or pleas'd repeat
 Thofe vows that won my foul to love.

DAMON.

D A M O N.

When o'er the mountain peeps the dawn,
 And round her ruddy beauties play,
I'll wake my Love to view the lawn,
 Or hear the warblers hail the day.
But, without thee, the rifing morn
 In vain awakes the cooling breeze,
In vain does nature's face adorn;
 Without my SYLVIA nought can pleafe.

S Y L V I A.

At night, when univerfal gloom
 Hides the bright profpect from our view,
When the gay groves give up their bloom,
 And verdant meads their lovely hue;
Tho' fleeting fpectres round me move,
 When in thy circling arms I'm preft,
I'll hufh my rifing fears with love,
 And fink in flumber on thy breaft.

D A M O N.

The new-blown rofe, whilft on its leaves
 Yet the bright fcented dew-drops found,
Pleas'd on thy bofom, whilft it heaves,
 Shall fhake its heav'nly fragrance round.
Then mingled fweets the fenfe fhall raife,
 Then mingled beauties catch the eye;
What pleafure on fuch charms to gaze!
 What rapture mid fuch fweets to lie!

SYLVIA.

SYLVIA.

How sweet thy words!—but, Damon ceafe,
   Nor strive to fix me ever here;
Too well you know thefe accents pleafe,
   That oft have fill'd my ravish'd ear.
Come, lead me to thefe promis'd joys,
   That dwelt fo lately on thy tongue;
Direct me by thy well known voice,
   And calm my tranfports with thy fong!

VERSES

Occafioned by a Young Lady's afking the Author,
What was a Cure for Love? 1758.

FROM me, my Dear, O feek not to receive
   What e'en deep-read Experience cannot give.
We may, indeed, from the Phyfician's fkill
Some Med'cine find to cure the body's ill.
But who e'er found the phyfic for the foul,
Or made th' affections bend to his controul?
When thro' the blaze of paffion objects fhow
How dark's the fhade! how bright the colours glow!
All the rous'd foul with tranfport's overcome,
And the mind's furly Monitor is dumb.

In vain the fages turn their volumes o'er,
And on the mufty page inceffant pore,

Still

Still mighty Love triumphant rules the heart,
Baffles their labour, and eludes their art.

Say what is fcience, what is reafon's force
To ftop the paffions wild ungovern'd courfe?
Reafon, 'tis true, may point the rocky fhore,
And fhew the danger, but can ferve no more,
From wave to wave the wretched wreck is toft,
And reafon 's in th' impetuous torrent loft.

In vain we ftrive, when urg'd by cold negle&,
By various means our freedom to effe&,
Tho' like the bee from fweet to fweet we rove,
And fearch for eafe in the vaft round of Love,
Tho' in each Nymph we meet a kind return,
Still in the firftfond hopelefs flame we burn,
That dear idea ftill our thoughts employs,
And bleft yariety itfelf e'en cloys.
So exiles banifh'd from their native home
Are met with pity wherefoe'er they come,
Yet ftill their native foil employs their care,
And death were eafe to lay their afhes there.

ODE

ODE

on FRIENDSHIP. 1758.

I.

FRIENDSHIP, all hail! thou deareſt tie,
   We Mortals here below can claim,
To blend our elſe unhappy lives with joy;
        My breaſt inſpire
        With thy true genuine fire,
        While to thy ſacred name,
        I ſtrike the golden lyre.
Cloath'd in pure empyrean light,
For vulgar eyes thou ſhin'ſt too bright;
        For while they gaze,
        Thy dazzling rays
Dim their too feeble ſight;
But ſouls uncloy'd with ſenſual toys,
Souls who ſeek true mental joys,
May Phœnix-like ſublimely ſoar,
May all thy heav'nly charms explore,
And wanton in the glorious blaze.

II.

  O G—*! if now no charming maid
Waits thy pencil's pow'rful aid,
That when her charms ſhall fade away,
And her pleaſing form decay;

                      That

That when her eyes no more ſhall roll,
Or heaving ſighs betray her ſoul;
           Still by thy art.
           The ſtubborn heart
To melt, and into love betray——
Attend! I ſing that pow'r divine,
Whoſe heav'nly influence ſways ſuch ſouls as thine——
Souls, by virtue made the ſame,
FRIENDSHIP's pow'rful ties may claim:
           And happy they,
           Without allay,
Bleſt in the gen'rous flame,

III.

Thus in his tent immur'd
           THETIS angry ſon,
Forgot the laurels he had won;
And whilſt love's flames his boſom burn'd,
His beauteous captive loſt he mourn'd;
And Ilium in his grief ſtood well ſecur'd:
All *Græcia's* chiefs diſmaid,
           Around him wait,
And vainly ſupplicate his aid.
Old *Neſtor's* eloquence was vain,
Ulyſſes cunning could not gain
The chief to draw his ſword.
           In angry ſtate,
           He ſullen ſate,
Nor deign'd to give a word.

IV.

But when PATROCLUS' much-lov'd fhade,
Pale, with blood and duft array'd,
Appear'd unto his view;
FRIENDSHIP fir'd his godlike breaft,
Conquer'd love the pow'r confeft,
And in a figh withdrew.
      Thus, the Ghoft——
" Attend, attend my call!
" Let not the vaunting *Trojans* boaft;
" But oh! revenge my fall."
With rage the Hero's bofom glows,
His blood in fwifter current flows;
See, how his eye.balls roll!
And fpeak the anguifh of his foul:
Revenge, revenge PATROCLUS cry'd:
      Quick at the word,
      He feiz'd his fword,
And clafp'd his feven-fold fhield;
Revenge, revenge, *Pelides* loud reply'd,
And rufh'd into the field.

V.

Wild as the wind he went
Thro' the aftonifh'd foe;
While death his fad concomitant,
Attends each fatal blow.
      With heaps of flain
      He ftrews the plain;

C   As

As when rough Boreas loudly blows,
Huge oaks and lofty pines around he throws,
Cowards revive when he appears,
And banish from their breasts their fears,
Nor death can more affright;
His presence ev'ry bosom warms,
They clank with horrid din their arms;
And with new courage fraught renew the fight,

     Now shouts around,
     And dying cries,
     A horrid found!
     Affail the skies,

And now the fainting *Trojans* yield
The long difputed honours of the field.

VI.

Round the field *Achilles* flies,
     For *Hector* he cries,
At length the *Trojan* chief efpies,
Horribly glorious midft the war;
Upon his bloody shield the God of day,
     Darts pendant rays;
     The crimson mirror far
     Reflects the blaze;
And all around him glories play.
PATROCLUS' mantle loofely flung,
The pledge of brave *Achilles*' love,
And by the fair *Ægina* wove;
Upon his manly shoulder hung.

The

VII.

The fatal fpoil *Achilles* fpies,
And indignation lightn'd in his eyes,
For friendfhip this, for friendfhip this, he faid,
And in his bofom drove the fhining blade.
Down the mighty *Dardan* fell,
   And in a groan exfpires;
Ill-fated *Ilium* gave a yell,
   And dreads her future fires.
In vain all-beauteous Venus ftrove
To ward the threatning blow;
   In vain fhe mov'd,
   In vain fhe lov'd
   Thofe raging fires,
   And wild defires,
To Friendfhip's purer flame muft bow.
Tho' Love the fenfual appetite,
   Tumultuous raife a while,
Friendfhip yields a calm delight,
   And will for ever fmile.

    EPISTLE

*EPISTLE

To a Friend ; from Fort HENRY.

Dated Auguſt 10, 1758.

FROM where his lofty head TALHEO rears,
   And o'er the wild in majeſty appears,
What ſhall I write that *——* won't diſcain,
Or worth, from Thee one moment's ſpace to gain ?
The Muſe, in vain, I court the lovely maid,
Views with contempt the rude unpoliſh'd ſhade,
Nor only this, ſhe flies fierce war's alarms,
And ſeeks where peace invites with ſofter charms;
Where the gay landſcapes ſtrike the travellers eyes,
And woods and lawns in beauteous order riſe ;
Where the glad Swain ſings on th' enamel'd green,
And views unaw'd by fears the pleaſing ſcene.
Here no enchanting proſpects yield delight,
But darkſome foreſts intercept the ſight;
Here fill'd with dread the trembling peaſants go,
And ſtart with terror at each nodding bough,
Nor as they trace the gloomy way along
Dare aſk the influence of a chearing ſong,

---

* Wrote, when the Author was, a Lieutenant in the Pennſylvania Forces, and, garriſoned at Fort HENRY. This little piece is the more valuable, as it contains a ſtriking picture, and perhaps the only one, of this kind, that will be preſerved, of the deep diſtreſs that overwhelmed our Frontier Settlements, when every field was ſtained with the blood of its Owners, by the mercileſs hands, of unfeeling Savages.

If

If in this wild a pleasing spot we meet,
In happier times some humble swain's retreat;
Where once with joy he saw the grateful soil
Yield a luxuriant harvest to his toil,
(Blest with content, enjoy'd his solitude,
And knew his pleasures, tho' of manners rude);
The lonely prospect strikes a secret dread,
While round the ravag'd Cott we silent tread,
Whose Owner fell beneath the savage hand,
Or roves a captive on some hostile land,
While the rich fields, with Ceres' blessings stor'd,
Grieve for their slaughter'd, or their absent lord.

Yet, would I now attempt, some sprightly strain,
And strive to wake your breast to mirth again,
Yet, would I call you from your Delia's urn,
But *Britain's* Genius bids her sons to mourn;
She shews the fatal field, all drench'd in gore,
And in sad accents cries, my *Howe's* no more!
Then let again the briny torrents flow,
Oh! teach your breast a nobler kind of woe!
To mourn *her* faded beauties now forbear,
And give the gallant Chief a *British* tear.

PASTORALS.

I.

To the fame.

BEFORE the rofy morn had broke the eaft,
Before the early lark had left her neft,
While yet the dewy damps of night hung round,
And all mankind were wrapt in fleep profound,
Two fwains whom facred Friendfhip and foft Love
Kept wakeful, 'rofe, and fought the filent grove;
His diftant Friend, caus'd youthful *Hylas'* care,
And am'rous *Damon* mourn'd his abfent Fair.

—— attend! e'er friendly to the Mufe,
Accept this trifle, and the faults excufe;
By genius fir'd, thy gen'rous breaft may claim
The fweets of Love, or Friendfhip's envied name.

Thus, as fair *Hylas* fung, the dales around,
Sad *Echo* play'd, and gave him back the found,
Ye fpotlefs ftreams, that plaintive glide along,
Be hufh'd a while, and liften to my fong;
Ye winged choirs that chanting on each tree,
Enliven ev'ry grove with melody.
Alexis' gone!—ceafe, ceafe to fwell your throats,
Harfh are you warblings as the raven's notes.

Droop, droop ye groves, ye plains in filence mourn,
Let nought be gay 'til *Alexis* return.

Here by my fide my pipe fhall ufelefs lay,
Unheeded now, *Alexis* is away.
In mourning here I will my time employ,
Nought fhall be feen that wears the face of joy.
Alexis' abfence here I will complain,
While the rude north-wind whiftles to my ftrain.
'Til he returns no more let fpring appear,
But hoary winter fhiver thro' the year.
Let mufic ceafe, let flow'rs no longer blow,
And murm'ring ftreams congeal'd, forget to flow.
  Droop, droop ye groves, ye plains in filence mourn,
  Let nought be gay 'til *Alexis* return.
How oft together Schuylkil's verdant fide
We've trac'd, or wanton'd in its cooling tide,
Or foft reclin'd, where fpreading fhades were wove,
With joyful accents fill'd the founding grove.
Then all was gay, then fprightly mirth was found,
And nature bloom'd in vernal beauties round.
Blow, blow ye winds, in fofteft breezes fend
My kindeft wifhes to my abfent Friend.
But ah! perhaps he heeds not, fome fweet maid
By artful wiles his youthful heart's betray'd,
Friendfhip perhaps is exil'd from his breaft,
By wanton love alone it is poffeft.
But, O ye maids, beware, none true can love,
Who e'er in holy Friendfhip faithlefs prove.
  Droop, droop ye groves, ye plains in filence mourn,
  Let nought be gay 'til *Alexis* return.

But fee, he comes, *Alexis* comes, found, found
The joyful news, let all the groves rebound.
Let forrow ceafe, let joy for ever reign,
Be nought but gladnefs feen throughout the plain;
He comes, *Alexis* comes, let all be gay,
And join with me to hail this happy day.
　　Ceafe now ye groves to droop, ye plains to mourn,
　　Let all be gay, *Alexis* doth return.

Then lovefick *Damon* thus, while all the grove
Refounds with *Delia's* name, and *Damon's* love.

How bright the view! how fragrant was the flow'r!
When beauty fmil'd, and *Delia* bleft the hour!
Her prefence then made ev'ry feafon gay,
And cold December bloom'd like vernal May.
Then rapture fill'd my fond exulting breaft,
And each intruding care was hufh'd to reft.
But now, alas! methinks the fhifted fcene
But only ferves to fhew how bleft I've been.
By her deferted, birds forget to fing,
And winter's dreary views deform the fpring.
All nature weeps, the lilly hangs its head,
The rofes fade, and mourning droops the mead.

Hie here, ye Nymphs, hie here, ye lovefick Swains,
Join in my woe, and aid my plaintive ftrains.

When

When on the plain I've tun'd my oaken reed,
While all around my bleating flock would feed,
In dumb attention seal'd, the liftning throng.
Hung on the found, and caught the pleafing fong;
Then loud applaufe my envied name would raife,
And diftant mountains *Echo* with my praife;
Then to the numbers *Delia's* voice was join'd,
And round my head the laurel wreath fhe twin'd.
But now in vain I ftrive for fkill, I've none,
My foul's untun'd, and flowing notes are gone.
  Hie here, ye Nymphs, hie here, ye lovefick Swains,
  Join in my woe, and aid my plaintive ftrains.

Fly fwift, ye hours, till fhe return again,
How flow they creep! ah! *Damon* 'tis in vain!
Time heeds thee not, nor will he fafter move,
Nor wing'd by fear, nor yet by fwifter love.
Slowly he brings us to the wonted joy,
But then how fwift the envied minutes fly!
All gracious heav'n, in pity lend the pow'r
To rule our paffions, or to guide the hour.
  Hie here, ye Nymphs, hie here, ye lovefick Swains,
  Join in my woe, and aid my plaintive ftrains.

II.

To Dr. J—— K——SL—Y, jun.

THE young *Alexis* drove his bleating Flock
     To the fea's fide, where feated on a rock,
That over-look'd the wave, in penfive mood
He threw his eyes along the azure flood;
His fadn'd brow well anxious care exprefs'd,
And oft the figh would heave his youthful breaft,
His flock neglected rang'd around him wide,
And ufelefs now his pipe hung by his fide.

     Calm was the fea, the fky appear'd ferene,
No angry ftorms deform'd the pleafing fcene;
Hufh'd in their caves the ruder winds were laid,
And only gentle weftern breezes play'd,
Gay beauty round feem'd blooming ev'ry where,
And the bright fcene half rob'd him of his care.
When a gay bark with fpreading fails difplay'd,
Appear'd to view, in garlands rich array'd.
Swift o'er the waves with eagle's fpeed fhe glides,
And fportive dolphins wanton'd by her fides,
Aloft in air the filken ftreamers flew,
While the fhrill mufic chear'd the jovial crew.

     Oh! thou, from whofe bleft fkill our bodies find
Sweet eafe, behold the ficknefs of the mind:

See, with what force, love fways the youthful heart,
Love, which ftill triumphs o'er thy heav'nly art.

Alexis thus—the feaman's life how bleft!
No anxious thoughts difturb his peaceful breaft.
Free as the wind from fhore to fhore he roves,
Taftes ev'ry fweet, and ev'ry blifs improves.
He wears no haughty beauty's fervile chain,
Nor heeds a Delia's frown or cold difdain;
Why was I form'd with fuch an abject mind,
Slave to a Fair the proudeft of her kind?

Then fudden all the heav'ns appear'd o'erfpread,
And the loud thunder fhook the Ocean's bed,
While ftreaming lightning dreadful fir'd the fky,
And the rough billows toft their heads on high:
Now to the heav'ns the giddy bark is rear'd,
And as fam'd Argo's rival there appear'd;
And then as fudden from th' amazing height
Sunk midft the watry vales, and fhun'd the fight;
While from her fhatter'd mafts the rude winds bear
Sails, cords and ftreamers, wildly thro' the air.

The Shepherd thus, ah! faithlefs cruel fea,
Thus *Delia* fmil'd, and thus fhe did betray.
Caught by the pleafing views, I left the fhore,
And gave my peace to feas untry'd before;
But foon, too foon the pleafing profpects fled,
And fwelling waves and tempefts did fucceed.

Witnefs, ye groves, and eke, ye pow'rs divine,
How oft fhe's fworn her faithlefs heart was mine.
Now, fir'd by female pride, fhe fcorns the truth,
And gives to wealthy *Ageon* her youth.
He's rich in num'rous flocks, fcarce knows his ftore,
My love is all, nor can I boaft of more.

How oft I've led her thro' the fhady grove,
While both our fouls feem'd join'd in mutual love!
Ah! then the Sirens foftnefs grac'd her tongue,
While quiv'ring on the pleafing founds I hung,
Such were the founds which 'woke the flumb'ring fhade,
Such were the founds which rais'd her from the dead!
Such were the founds of *Amphion's* charming lyre,
And fuch the mufic of the heav'nly quire!

How oft when feated by the chryftal flood,
Pleas'd would we captivate the finny brood!
There in the floating mirror would I trace
Each ftriking beauty of her angel face,
Her cheek embellifh'd with the rofy die,
Her ruby lip, and heav'nly fparkling eye,
'Til fome rude wind would o'er the furface pafs,
And envious fnatch the beauteous mimic face.
How great the change!——— and then he ftarting fpy'd
Her body floating on the boift'rous tide.
And by the charmer's fide the wild waves bore,
Still link'd in death, *Ageon* to the fhore.

But,

But, oh! how fill'd with terror at the fight!
His eyes were veil'd in endlefs fhades of night.
Cold was her breaft, quick fleeting life had fled,
And on her faded cheeks the rofe lay dead.
Fix'd like a figur'd ftone awhile he ftood,
And gave the tear with anguifh to the flood;
Then frantic clafp'd her midft the briny lave,
And dafh'd with anger each intruding wave:
He eager preft her lips, now pale and wet,
But for his warmth a deadly coldnefs met;
Tho' once with ruby luftre bright they fhone,
Their glow was loft, and all their fweetnefs gone.
Now welcome death, the lovefick Shepherd cry'd,
And fainting on her clay-cold bofom dy'd.

III.

To the Memory of GENERAL WOLFE,

who was flain at the taking of QUEBEC.

SET was the Sun, and from her filver throne
With fainter luftre pallid Cynthia fhone,
O'er the wide world, and round th' etherial plain
Old dufky Night had fpread her gloomy reign;
When *Lyfidas* was by *Damætas* found
In a dark grove, ftretch'd on the dewy ground,
In filence firft his wonder he exprefs'd,
And thus, at length, the mournful Swain addrefs'd.

DAMÆTAS.

DAMÆTAS.

Why refts, my *Lyfidas*, beneath this fhade?
See all around night's fable curtain's fpread:
Hafte, hafte away pale ghofts are feen around,
And troops of elves in ev'ry glade abound;
For prey the hungry woodland tyrant roves,
And horror fhadows all the deepning groves.
As thro' the glade I halloo'd to thine ear,
Fierce wolves reply'd, and fil'd my foul with fear.

LYSIDAS.

Ah! leave me, leave me to this deep recefs,
Fit is this gloom for forrows and diftrefs.

DAMÆTAS.

Thy flocks are fafe, I faw them to the fold,
'Ere parting day had ting'd the weft with gold,
Thy *Chloris* too I met, as o'er the plain
She fought the cottage of her much-lov'd Swain.
What forrows fay can now ufurp that breaft
Where love and gayety were wont to reft?
Oh! fpeak, and let thy lov'd *Damætas* know,
Who oft thy joy partakes fhould fhare thy woe.

LYSIDAS.

How kindly urg'd! then gentle Shepherd hear,
Nor ftop the figh, nor hold the gufhing tear;
And yet, as I attempt the fadning tale,
My ftronger forrows o'er my pow'rs prevail;
Such too will be thy forrows when I've faid,
The firft of Shepherds, brave *Amintor*'s dead.

DAMÆTAS.

DAMÆTAS.

Amintor dead!——then feated on the ground
Here by thy fide, let fpectres gleam around;
Let wayward elves here dance their magic ring,
And night around us double horrors bring.
Here will I fit until her fable noon,
And aid the wolves to bay the wandring moon;
Tho' fickning dews and damps around my head
With falling ftars, their baleful influence fhed.

LYSIDAS.

Oh! Shepherd oft I've heard thy pleafing ftrain,
Like *Philomel* in gentle woe complain.
Our flocks attentive to thy wond'rous reed,
Left the clear ftream, and quite forgot to feed.
Come then, once more with mufick fill the glade,
And waken airy *Echo* in her fhade.
Such as when, at *Menalcas* death your fong,
Fix'd in attention all the liftning throng.

DAMÆTAS.

'Twas thy fuperior fkill from *Codrus'* bore
The prize, two lambkins from his fleecy ftore,
Nor is *Alexis'* ftrain fo fweet as thine,
Altho' the boafted fav'rite of the Nine.
'Tis true my pipe has oft-times on the plain
Pleas'd the gay Nymph and chear'd the active Swain.
But fince *Menalcas'* death here by my fide,
My reed, his gift, has ftill remain'd untry'd.

LYSIDAS.

LYSIDAS.

Then let us here, 'til early morn's return,
Join both our fkills, and teach the night to mourn;
I'll ftretch my utmoft art to aid thy lays,
And happy me could I obtain thy praife.

DAMÆTAS.

Ah! now I know, why threatning flam'd on high,
Bright blazing comets dreadful in the fky.
Our Sages fhook their heads, and fear'd to tell
The future evil, which they knew full well.
Two moons are wafted fince beneath this fhade ⎫
As to our Shepherds on my reed I play'd, ⎬
With weary fteps old *Arcos* hither ftray'd. ⎭
Thus fpoke the Sire, here forrow foon fhall reign,
No longer joy fhall dwell upon the plain,
Corroding care fhall banifh peaceful reft,
And pain and anguifh feize on ev'ry breaft.
I laugh'd in gayety to hear the Sire
Speak what I thought his dotage did infpire.
But now I know what caus'd his mighty dread,
The firft of Shepherds, brave *Amintor*'s dead.

LYSIDAS.

When ruffian Robbers, e'er in rapine bold,
Veil'd in the fhade of night wou'd break our fold,
Amintor firft was ever to purfue,
And ne'er in vain his threatning arrows flew.

Oft

Oft in their gore the midnight plunderers lay,
Oppress'd with spoil, and sigh'd their souls away;
But now far hence is smiling safety fled,
Since brave *Amintor*, first of Swains, is dead.

DAMÆTAS.

E'er fond of danger, eager in the chace,
With fearless mind he fought the savage race;
Foremost to dare, he still with gallant pride
First clomb the cliff, or rush'd into the tide;
'Til smear'd in glorious horror with the gore,
Of the fierce Tiger or the foaming Boar,
At eve returning from the dang'rous toil
He o'er his shoulders spread the shagged spoil.
Our Shepherds met him with a loud acclaim,
And ev'ry Coward's cheek was mark'd with shame.
But now unaw'd the Savage Tyrants tread
The silent grove, for brave *Amintor*'s dead.

LYSIDAS.

The sorrowing Mother met the mournful bier,
Loose on her neck flow'd her dishevel'd hair;
Around her all her weeping Daughters stood,
And wash'd his wounds with tears, a briny flood.
Oft times she sigh'd, and beat her aged breast,
And loud complaints her inward woe exprest.
Thus spake the Dame, ye tuneful Shepherds come,
And hang your deathless ditties round his tomb;

E   Here

Here all around your flow'ry garlands throw,
And on his grave let ſhort-liv'd roſes blow.
Haſte here, ye Swains, here let your tears be ſhed,
Weep Shepherds, weep, the brave *Amintor*'s dead.
So ſung the Swains, 'til Phœbus' radiant light,
Chac'd to her azure bed the Queen of Night.

---

* A DITHYRAMBIC
on WINE.

I.

COME! let Mirth our hours employ,
  The jolly God inſpires;
The roſy juice our boſom fires,
And tunes our ſouls to joy.
See, great *Bacchus* now deſcending,
Gay, with bluſhing honours crown'd;
Sprightly *Mirth* and *Love* attending,
    Around him wait,
    In ſmiling ſtate——
    Let *Echo* reſound,
    Let *Echo* reſound
    The joyful news all around.

---

* The DITHYRAMBIC demands a greater boldneſs than any other poetical compoſition, and is indeed the only one in which a lyric irregularity may be happily indulged.
Francis's HORACE.

As our Poet appears ſo warm on his ſubject, it may not be amiſs to remark here, that *he never drank any Wine*, and that his *bumpers* are all *ideal*, which may ſerve, perhaps, as a refutation of that noted adage, that *a water drinker can never be a good Dithyrambic Poet*.

Fond

II.

Fond Mortals come, if love perplex,
In *Wine* relief you'll find;
Who 'd whine for womens giddy fex
More fickle than the wind?
If beauty's bloom thy fancy warms,
Here, fee her fhine,
Cloath'd in fuperior charms;
More lovely than the blufhing morn,
When firft the op'ning day
Bedecks the thorn,
And makes the meadows gay.
Here fee her in her cryftal fhrine;
See and adore; confefs her all divine,
The Queen of Love and Joy.
Heed not thy Chloe's fcorn——
  This fparkling glafs,
  With winning grace,
Shall ever meet thy fond embrace,
And never, never, never cloy,
  No never, never cloy.

III.

Here, POET! fee, *Caftalia's* fpring——
Come, give me a bumper, I'll mount to the fkies,
Another, another——'Tis done! I arife;
  On fancy's wing,
  I mount, I fing,
  And now, fublime,

      Parnaffus'

Parnaſſus' lofty top I climb——
But hark ! what ſounds are theſe I hear,
Soft as the dream of her in love,
Or *Zephyr's* whiſp'ring thro' the Grove?
And now, more ſolemn far than fun'ral woe,
The heavy numbers flow !
   And now again,
   The varied ſtrain,
Grown louder and bolder, ſtrikes quick on the ear,
And thrills thro' ev'ry vein.

    IV.

'Tis *Pindar's* ſong !
His ſofter notes the fanning gales
Waft acroſs the ſpicy vales,
   While, thro' the air,
   Loud whirlwinds bear
The harſher notes along.
   Inſpir'd by *Wine*,
He leaves the lazy croud below,
Who never dar'd to peep abroad,
And, mounting to his native ſky,
For ever there ſhall ſhine.
   No more I'll plod
   The beaten road ;
Like him inſpir'd, like him I'll mount on high;
   Like his my ſtrain ſhall flow.

            Haſte;

V.

Hafte, ye Mortals! leave your forrow;
Let pleafure crown to day————to morrow
   Yield to fate.
Join the univerfal chorus,
   Bacchus reigns,
    Ever great;
   Bacchus reigns
    Ever glorious————
Hark! the joyful groves rebound,
Sporting breezes catch the found,
And tell to hill and dale around————
   " *Bacchus* reigns "————
    While far away,
The bufy *Echoes* die away.————

THE WISH.

I ONLY afk a mod'rate fate,
 And tho' not in obfcurity,
I would not yet be plac'd too high;
Between the two extreames I'd be,
Not meanly low, nor yet too great,
From both contempt and envy free.

With

If no glitt'ring wealth I have,
Content of bounteous heav'n I crave,
For that is more,
Than all the India's fhining ftore,
To be unto the duft a flave.
With heart, my little I will ufe,
Nor let pain my life devour,
Or for a griping heir refufe
Myfelf one pleafant hour.

No ftately Edifice to rear,
My Wifh would bound a fmall retreat,
In temp'rate air, and furnifh'd neat;
No ornaments would I prepare,
No coftly labours of the loom,
Should e'er adorn my humble room;
To gild my roof, I nought require
But the ftern Winter's friendly fire.

Free from tumultuous cares and noife,
If gracious heav'n my Wifh would give,
While fweet content augments my joys,
Thus, my remaining hours I'd live.
By arts ignoble never rife,
The Mifer's ill-got wealth defpife;
But bleft my leifure hours I'd fpend,
The Mufe enjoying, and my Friend.

A

A NIGHT-PIECE.

HOW awful is the Night! beneath whofe fhade,
 Calm mournful filence e'er ferenely reigns;
And mufing Meditation, heav'nly Maid!
 Unbends the mind, and fooths the heart-felt pains!

II.

What pleafing terrors ftrike upon the foul
 While hills and vales around dufk fwims away;
While murmuring ftreams in plaintive numbers roll,
 And with their foft complainings clofe the day!

III.

While filver Cynthia, with her pallid beams,
 Does clouded nature faintly re-illume,
Tips tops of trees, and dancing on the ftreams,
 Adds livelier horror to the rifing gloom!

IV.

What hand can picture forth the folemn fcene,
 The deepning fhade and the faint glimm'ring light!
How much above th' expreffive art of * G—n
 Are the dim beauties of the dewy night!

V.

How much this hour does noify day excel
 To thofe who heav'nly contemplation love!——
Now nought is hear'd but penfive *Philomel*
 The wat'ry fall, or *Zephyr* in the grove.

----

* Mr. JOHN GREEN, an ingenious Portrait Painter, a particular friend of Mr. GODFREY'S,
and Author of the Elegy, that precedes thefe POEMS, on Mr. G's death.

Now

VI.

Now fearching thought unlimited may rove,
  And into nature's deep receffes pry;
Spread her fleet wings to mount the realms above, *
  And gain the glowing glories of the fky.

VII.

Rich in expreffion, how fublimely bright,
  Thofe lucent arguments above us fhine!
Now, Atheift! now lift up thy wondring fight,
  And own the great creating pow'r divine.

VIII.

Heav'ns! what a throng, what a dread endlefs train,
  Of complicated wonders yield furprize!
Syftems on fyftems, fyftems yet again,
  And funs on funs, continually arife!

IX.

Too daring thought! give o'er thy vain emprize,
  Nor rafhly pry——at humble diftance gaze!
Should heav'n unveil thofe beauties to our eyes
  The dazzled fenfe would fink beneath the blaze.

X.

But leave the glories of heav'n's fpangl'd dome,
  And thy flow-fteps to dreary church-yards lead;
There lean attentive on yon marble tomb,
  And learn inftruction from the filent dead.

How

XI.

How difmal is this place! whilft round I gaze,
    What chilling fears my thoughtful foul invade!
Exaggerating Fancy fhrubs doth raife,
    To dreadful fpectres gliding crofs the fhade.

XII.

Pale fleep! thou emblem of eternal reft,
    When lock'd in thy coercive ftrong embrace,
Thofe of all-bounteous Nature's gifts poffeft,
    Are but as thofe whofe gloomy haunts I trace.

XIII.

No objects now wide-ftraining eyes admit;
    Deaf is the ear, mute the perfuafive tongue,
Difcerning judgment; and keen piercing wit
    Are loft in thee, aud warriors nerves unftrung!

XIV.

Still led by thee imagination roves,
    On tow'ring pinion feeks fome diftant world;
Or wanders pleas'd thro' foft enamel'd groves,
    Or down the dreadful precipice is hurl'd.

XV.

While fad reclining on this filent tomb,
    Surrounded with promifcuous dead I reft;
Thee, I invoke! fweet friendly fleep, O come!
    Lock up my fenfe, and lull my troubl'd breaft!

F

The

THE
COURT of FANCY;

A POEM.

The Poet's eye, in a fine frenzy rolling,
Doth glance from heaven to earth, from earth to heav'n;
And, as imagination bodies forth
The forms of things unknown, the Poet's pen
Turns them to shape, and gives to aiery nothing
A local habitation and a name.

SHAKESPEAR.

The learned reader need not be acquainted that the Author took the hint of the Tranſition from the Court of Fancy to that of Deluſion, from Chaucer's Poem called the Houſe of Fame, where the change is from the Houſe of Fame to that of Rumour; and that he likewiſe had Mr. Pope's beautiful Poem on that ſubject in his eye, at the Time when he compos'd this Piece.

THE
COURT of FANCY.

'TWAS fultry noon, impatient of the heat
 I fought the covert of a clofe retreat:
Soft by a bubbling fountain was I laid,
And o'er my head the fpreading branches play'd;
When gentle flumber ftole upon my eyes,   5.
And bufy *Fiction* bid this vifion rife.

Methought I penfive unattended ftood,
Wrapt in the horrors of a defert wood;
Old Night and Silence fpread their fway around,
And not a breeze difturb'd the dread profound.   10
To break the wild, and gain the neighb'ring plain
Oft I effay'd, and oft effay'd in vain;
Still in intricate mazes round I run,
And ever ended where I firft begun.
While thus I lab'ring ftrove t' explore my way,   15
Bright on my fenfe broke unexpected Day:
Retiring Night in hafte withdrew her fhade,
And fudden morn fhone thro' the op'ning glade.
No more the fcene a defert wild appear'd,
A fmiling grove its vernal honors rear'd;   20

While

While fweetnefs on the balmy breezes hung,
And all around a joyful Mattin rung.
Soft was the ftrain as *Zephyr* in the grove,
Or purling ftreams that thro' the meadows rove.
Now wild in air the varying ftrain is toft,　　　　　　25
In diftant echoes then the found is loft;
Again reviv'd, and lo! the willing trees
Rife to the pow'rful numbers by degrees.
Trees now no more, robb'd of their verdant bloom,
They fhine fupporters of a fpacious dome,　　　　　　30
The wood to bright tranfparent cryftal chang'd,
High fluted columns rife in order rang'd.

So to the magic of *Amphion's* lyre
Stones motion found, and *Thebes* was feen t' afpire;
The nodding forefts 'rofe with the foft found,　　　　　35
And gilded turrets glitter'd all around:
Each wond'ring God bent from his heav'nly feat
To view what pow'rful mufic cou'd compleat.

High on a mountain was the pile difclos'd,
And fpreading limes th' afcending walks compos'd;　　　40
While far below the waving woods declin'd,
Their verdant tops bow'd with the gentle wind.
Bright varying *Novelty* produc'd delight,
And *Majefty* and *Beauty* charm'd the fight.
Such are the fcenes which *Poets* fweetly fing,　　　　45
By *Fancy* taught to ftrike the trembling ftring.

Here

Here *Fancy's* fane, near to the bleft abode
Of all her kindred Gods, fuperior ftood.
Dome upon dome it fparkl'd from on high,
Its lofty top loft in the azure fky.   50
By *Fiction's* hand th' amazing pile was rear'd,
In ev'ry part ftupendous fkill appear'd ;
In beautiful diforder yet compleat,
The ftructure fhone irregular and great :
The noble frontispiece of antique mold   55
Glitter'd with gems, and blaz'd with burnifh'd gold.

  Now thro' the founding vaults, felf op'ning rung
The maffy gates on golden hinges hung ;
All the bright ftructure was difclos'd to view,
Magnificent with beauty ever new !   60
Trembling I ftood abforb'd in dread furprize,
And fudden glory dim'd my aching eyes.
Unnumber'd Pillars all around were plac'd,
Their capitals with artful fculpture grac'd.
Wide round the roof a fictious fky was rais'd,   65
A glorious Sun in the meridian blaz'd,
On the rich columns play'd his dazzling ray,
And all around diffuf'd immortal day ;
A fhining Phœnix on th' effufive rays
Fix'd his afpiring eye with fteady gaze.   70
Beneath appear'd a chequer'd pavement, bright
With fparkling Jafpanyx and Chryfolite.

                                                     'Round

'Round, by creating *Fiction's* hand renew'd,
Gay vifionary fcenes in order ftood;
Th' obedient figures at her touch difclos'd,
And various tales the glowing walls compos'd.

Here mighty *Jove* amidft affembl'd Gods,
Rais'd on his ftarry Throne majeftic nods;
On his right hand the dreadful fates are feen,
And on his left is plac'd his haughty *Queen.*
There the pale *Tyrant* of the dreary coafts
Sways with his pow'rful fceptre fleeting ghofts.
Blue *Neptune* fcours along his wat'ry reign,
Now lifts the waves aloft now ftils the raging main.
Perch'd on a lofty rock *Æolus* ftands,
And holds the winds in ftrong coercive bands.
Here the bright *Queen* of beauty ftands confefs'd,
There angry *Mars* in martial honors drefs'd.
Alcides here appears with warrior pride,
The Lion's fpoil defcending o'er his fide,
The watchful Dragon at his feet is lain,
The Lernean Hydra and dire Centaurs flain.
Here glows *Diana* eager in the chace,
And there *Minerva* fhews with fober grace.
There with the madning rout clofe at his heels,
Young *Bacchus,* jolly God, triumphant reels.
Gay *Maia's* fon high mounted on the wind,
Cuts thro' the air and leaves the clouds behind.

Toward the rofy Eaft, great *Mithra* fhone,
Bright in the glories of a rifing fun.   100
Beneath in folemn pomp with hands uprear'd,
In flowing robes the Magi all appear'd.
Here the fage * *Baƈtrian* pois'd his magic wand,
Obedient *Genii* waited his command.
There *Thammuz* laid, while from the gaping wound   105
Pour'd the rich ftream, and fanguin'd all the ground.
Amidft his impious vot'ries *Chemos'* ftood,
And horrid *Moloch* fmear'd with infant blood.

Northward fierce *Woden* ftood with terrors crown'd,
And angry *Thor* threw heedlefs thunder round.   110
Fair *Friga* with her lovely train was feen,
The beauteous rival of the paphian Queen.
Old *Merlin* ftruck the' lyre, the wond'ring throng
Attended 'round to his prophetic fong.

Southward diforder'd figures ftruck my eyes,   115
Monkies and *Serpents* rais'd to deities;
Mad fuperftitious *Ægypt* thefe rever'd
And to the hideous tribe their pray'rs prefer'd.
Maim'd *Memnon* there feem'd on his harp to play,
And hail *Ofiris* bringing on the day.   120
Pale *Ifis* crefcent faintly glimmer'd here,
And barking *Anubis* difplay'd the year.

---

* *Zoroafter.*

G

Gay sportive fawns adorn'd the distant scene,
In antic measures skipping o'er the green.
There sea Nymphs wanton'd on the wat'ry gleam,   125
Rode on the waves, or cleav'd the yielding stream.
Here the pale *Sybils* rang'd their mystic leaves,
And *Ætna* with the lab'ring *Cyclops* heaves.
There craggy rocks the sons of *Titan* tore,   }
And mountains shaggy roots tremendous bore,   } 130
And threat'n'd *Jove* with the promiscuous war. }

Bold *Phæton* here urg'd his mad request,
Ambitious joy swell'd his presumtuous breast;
Elate he mounted in the flaming car,
The Sire attended with a fix'd despair;   135
Nor could the Parent's tears the Youth restrain,
He laugh'd at fear, and daring took the rein.
The fiery steeds his feeble hand despise,
And stretch'd with glowing ardor thro' the skies;
Now thunders roll'd, pale lightning play'd around,   140
And the rash boy soon felt the burning wound.

Pygmalion there the statue seem'd to move,
Assisted by the pow'rful Queen of Love;
With rapture fir'd, to his exulting breast
The animated stone he fondly prest;   145
Transported on each shining feature gaz'd,
Now soften'd into life, and saw amaz'd,
Awaken'd into sense, her eye-balls roll,
And heaving breasts bespoke the ent'ring soul;

Saw

Saw on her cheeks the rofy tinƈture burn,   150
And felt her lips the ravifh'd kifs return.

Fam'd *Dædalus* here wing'd the midway air,
And fighing, faw his Son difdain his care.
Young *Icarus* on fpreading pinions rofe,
And fcorn'd the path his wary Sire had chofe ;   155
For heav'n the afpiring Boy his flight begun,
But felt the ardor of too near a Sun ;
The temper'd wax before the fcorching Ray
Melted, and lo ! the loofen'd wings gave way ;
And while his father's Name his accents gave,   160
Fell from the height, and funk beneath the wave.

Diana's rage there haplefs *Aƈteon* feels,
And faw his hounds purfuing at his heels ;
Chang'd to a Stag, he fwept along the plain,
In vain his fpeed, he flew from death in vain.   165

Elyfium next difclos'd its blifsful bow'rs,
With heav'nly fruitage deck'd, and radiant flow'rs ;
Celeftial *Amaranth* eternal bloom'd,
And the bright Plains with od'rous fcents perfum'd ;
Thro' the gay Meads an amber current roll'd   170
O'er fands refplendent as *Arabia*'s gold,
On whofe green banks the happy Shades reclin'd,
Quafft its fweet ftream, and left their cares behind.

What ever Dreamer dreamt, or Poet fung,
Or lying Fable with her double tongue   175
Told the believing World, now did appear
Delufions all, for when approaching near
They fhun'd the view, and fhrunk to empty Air.

High in the midft, rais'd on her rolling throne,
Sublimely eminent bright FANCY fhone.   * 180
A glitt'ring * Tiara her temples bound,
Rich fet with fparkling Rubies all around;
Her azure eyes roll'd with majeftic grace,
And youth eternal bloom'd upon her face,
A radiant bough, Enfign of her command,   185
Of polifh'd gold wav'd in her lilly hand;
The fame the Sybil to *Æneas* gave,
When the bold *Trojan* crofs'd the Stygian wave.
In filver traces fix'd unto her Car,
Four fnowy Swans, proud of th'imperial Fair,   190
Wing'd lightly on, each in gay beauty dreft,
Smooth'd the foft plumage that adorn'd her breaft.
Sacred to her the lucent Chariot drew,
Or whether wildly thro' the air fhe flew,
Or whether to the dreary fhades of Night   195
Opprefs'd with gloom fhe downwards bent her flight,
Or proud afpiring fought the bleft abodes,
And boldly fhot among th'affembl'd Gods.

---

* This Conceit is occafioned, by the Tiara's being a Badge of Royalty ufed in the Eaft, and the oriental Writers abounding much in Pieces of Imagination.

On

On her right hand appear'd the joyful Nine,
And on her left the Graces all ˜divine;   200
Young Infant *Love* foft ˜on her breaft reclin'd,
And with his Mother's glowing beauty fhin'd.
Her fav'rite Sons were rang'd in Order round,
In three bright bands with deathlefs lawrels crown'd ;
Great *Homer* here enjoy'd fuperior day,   205
Illuminated by bright Fancy's ray;
Apelles there, whofe magic hand could give
Form to the mafs, and bid the fiction live ;
Timotheus next, whofe animated Lyre
Cold Grief could charm, and thoughtlefs rage infpire.   210

Clofe at her feet a Bard in raptures loft
Was plac'd, and wildly round his eye-balls toft ;
Great Fancy was the theme ! the foothing ftrain
In floods of pleafure thrill'd thro' ev'ry vein.
Thus, while the trembling notes afcend on high,   215
He fung; Indulgent Queen of ev'ry joy,
What rapture fills the breaft thou doft infpire,
The Lover's tranfport, and the Poet's fire !
At thy command obedient Pleafure bends,
And rofy Beauty to thy call attends ;   220
The fanning gales fhall fwelling fpread thy fame,
And echoing Groves well-pleas'd refound thy Name !

While thus around my eyes I wildly threw,
From charm to charm, and did each wonder view,

Pleas'd

Pleas'd on the heav'nly ravifhment to gaze,   225
'Rofe with the ftrain, or wanton'd in the blaze !
Her awful Silence the bright Goddefs broke,
And frowning, thus in angry mood fhe fpoke.
Com'ft thou, vain Mortal, here with fearching Eye
Into the fecrets of our Court to pry ?   230
What rafh prefumption fwells thy youthful breaft,
That in our prefence thus you've rudely preft ?

   Trembling I kneel'd, with fear my tongue was ty'd
A fpace, when fpeech regain'd, I thus reply'd.
With lowly Rev'rence I hither came,   235
Not to deride, but to adore thy Name ;
To thee I ever dedicate my Song,
To hail thy glories 'midft this fuppliant throng.

   Then from her fhining feat, the heav'nly Maid
In beautiful arrifion, anfw'ring faid ;   240
Then have thy wifh, here Mortal take this Lyre,
Strike bold the ftrings, and fing as I infpire.
Humbly I bow'd, her mild commands obey'd,
And carelefs o'er the Lyre my fingers laid,
And foon with wild poetic rage poffefs'd,   245
All my frame fhook, and lab'ring heav'd my breaft.
By Fancy fir'd, enraptur'd thus I fung,
Whilft all around redoubling Echoes rung.

                        Zephyr

Zephyr attend, or whether thro' the grove
Soft whisp'ring you the leafy branches move, 250
Or shaking dulcet dew-drops from each flow'r
Wide thro' the plain you spread the fragrant show'r,
Or whether *Sylvia* panting in some shade
In tender accents woos thee to her aid!
No more in am'rous sporting spend the day, 255
No longer wanton on her bosom play:
Fancy commands! obey the regal Fair,
Fancy commands! quick all your wings prepare!
From the Sun's early dawn till where again
He sets his glories in the azure main; 260
Thro' ev'ry Clime her royal mandate bear,
And bid mankind to her bright Court repair.
Hear Earth's Inhabitants! ye Mortals hear!
And let attentive wonder fix each ear.
Fancy invites! nor let her ask in vain, 265
Come, taste her heav'nly sweets, and hail her reign!

Zephyr obedient on his wings convey'd
The joyful Summons warbling thro' the glade,
Swiftly he swept along the spicy vale,
Caught all its sweets, and in a balmy gale 270
Gently he stole on the fond Lover's ear,
And in loud accents bid the Warrior hear!
From diff'rent Climes the thronging Nations came,
And rush'd promiscuously before the Dame;

Prostrate

Proſtrate before her throne their hands they rear, ·   275
And to the Goddeſs loud prefer their pray'r.
Confus'd they all demand her promis'd joys,
While the long vaults refound their clam'rous noiſe.
As when loud billows break upon the ſhore,
Or o'er th' oppoſing Rocks the torrents roar.   280
Her glitt'ring branch impatient round ſhe ſwung,
And inſtant ſilence ſeiz'd each babbling tongue.
Abaſh'd they trembling ſtood, and ſeem'd to be
Transfix'd in mute inſenſibility.
Quick was diſpers'd each wild tumultuous ſound,   285
And the ſoft breezes all were huſh'd around.

Now ſwiftly forward falſe Deluſion came,
Wrapt in a fulvid Cloud appear'd the Dame.
Thin was her form, in airy garments dreſt,
And groteſque figures flam'd upon her veſt ;   290
In her right hand ſhe held a magic glaſs,
From whence around reflected glories paſs.
Blind by the ſubtle rays, the giddy Croud
Ruſh'd wildly from the Dome and ſhouted loud.
The few remain'd whom Fancy did inſpire   295
Yet undeceiv'd by vain Deluſion's fire.

A Troop of ſhining forms the next came on,
Foremoſt bright Nature's awful Goddeſs ſhone.
Fair *Truth* ſhe led, in ſpotleſs white array'd,
And pleaſing *Beauty*, ſweet celeſtial Maid ;   300

Where

Where *Truth* and *Nature* aid the great defign,
Beauty attends, and makes it all divine.

Sweet *Poefy* was feen their fteps behind,
With golden treffes fporting in the wind;
In carelefs plaits did her bright garments flow,   305
And nodding laurels wav'd around her brow;
Sweetly fhe ftruck the ftring, and fweetly fung,
Th' attentive tribe on the foft accents hung.
'Tis her's to fing who great in arms excel,
Who bravely conquer'd or who glorious fell;   310
Heroes in verfe ftill gain a deathlefs name,
And ceafelefs ages their renown proclaim.
Oft to Philofophy fhe lends her aid,
And treads the Sage's folitary fhade;
Her great firft tafk is nobly to infpire   315
Th' immortal Soul with Virtue's facred fire.

Then *Painting* forward mov'd in garlands dreft,
The Rainbows varied tints adorn'd her veft.
Great Nature's Rival!——quick to her command
Beauty attends, and aids her pow'rful hand.   320
At her creative touch gay fictions glow,
Bright Tulips bloom, and op'ning Rofes blow.
The canvafs fee, what pleafing profpects rife!
What varying Beauty ftrikes our wond'ring eyes!
Chill'd Winter's waftes, or Spring's delightful green,   325
Hot Summer's pride, or Autumn's yellow fcene;

H   Here

Here lawns are fpread, there tow'ring forefts wave,
The heights we fear, or wifh the cooling lave !

Her blooming Sifter in her hand fhe led,
Joy in her eye, fair *Sculpture* heav'n taught Maid.   330
'Tis her's to ftone a mimic life to give,
Heroes and Sages at her call revive ;
See flow'ry Orators with out-ftretch'd hand
Addrefs'd to fpeak, in glowing marble ftand !

Sudden I hear'd foft founds, a pleafing ftrain!   335
Mufic advanc'd with all her heav'nly train. .
Sweetly enraptur'd then my pulfe beat high,
And my breaft glow'd fraught with unufual joy.
'Tis harmony can ev'ry paffion move,
Give forrow eafe, or melt the foul to love ;   340
Exulting Pleafure to her call attends,
E'en ftormy Rage to pow'rful mufic bends.

With Turrets crown'd bright *Architecture* fhone,
The lovely Maid with eafy fteps came on ;
Graceful her mien, her looks celeftial fhin'd,   345
Where majefty and foftning beauty join'd.
At her command fee lofty Piles afcend,
Columns afpire, triumphal Arches bend.

Aftronomy with proud afpiring Eye,
Gaz'd on the glowing beauties of the fky.   350

Her

Her veſt with glitt'ring Stars was ſpangl'd o'er,
And in her hand a Teleſcope ſhe bore.
With this ſhe mark'd the rolling Planets way,
Or where portentous Comets dreadful ſtray.

Tho' laſt, not leaſt *Philoſophy* was ſeen,   355
Slow was her ſtep, and awful was her mien;
A Volume open in her hand ſhe held,
With Nature's law the ample page was fill'd.
'Tis her's great Nature's wond'rous depths t' explore,
Or to the Gods in heav'nly rapture ſoar.   360

With *theſe* bright *Fancy's* Sons their hours employ,
Purſue *their* lore, and taſte each riſing joy.

Now ſuddenly the ſcene was chang'd again,
And brought to view Deluſion's ſpreading reign:
There intermingl'd hills and rocks were ſeen,   365
Here ſhady Groves and flow'ry Lawns between.
Full in the front a lofty Pile was rear'd,
The Architecture old and rude appear'd.
Deluſion's reſidence, within confin'd
Gay Fictions lurk, and Dreams of ev'ry kind.   370
Conſtant as waters roll, or flames aſcend,
Hither their courſe the riſing vapours bend;
Dreſt by her hand they ſhine with mimic bloom,
Or at her word their nothingneſs reſume.

But

But ftill from *Fancy* all her pow'r fhe draws,   375
Bows to her Name, and owns her facred Laws.
Some in light Dreams the fleeping fenfes move,
And led by them the thoughts unfettl'd rove,
Others more bold majeftic portments take,
And plague delighted thofe who dream awake.   380
Such are the dreams of thofe who thirft for pow'r,
The fuperftitious, and a thoufand more.
Others ufurp the features of the Dead,
And fhake the torch around the Murth'rer's bed;
Affright the Vigil, or in wanton mirth   385
Make fools feek hidden treafures in the earth,
Or lead the weary traveller awry,
Or rifing flame amazement in the fky.

  Now with the croud Delufion forward came,
A Troop of Phantoms flutter'd round the Dame;   390
In bands the throng fhe inftantly divides,
A Phantom over ev'ry band prefides.

  Foremoft a bright majeftic Form appear'd,
And in her hand the honour'd Fafces rear'd;
Forward fhe ftrode with more than virgin pace,   395
And leer'd upon the Croud with haughty grace.
Power was her name, affuming felfifh Pride
And glitt'ring Pomp attended by her fide.
Her fav'rite Son high on a feat fhe plac'd,
With mimic gems and glaffy bawbles grac'd;   400
Clofe

Clofe by his fide was feated wrinkl'd Care,
While Envy view'd him with malicious ftare:
Sternly he ey'd around the fervile throng,
While loud acclaim proceeded from each tongue;
But from the giddy height devolving foon,   405
Reproach, Contempt and Shame is on him thrown.
Eager another mounts the chair of pow'r,
And fhines the empty pageant of an hour.

Dame *Superftition* was the next came on,
Bright on her head the gilded mitre fhone,   410
Varying her afpect, now fhe rais'd her eye,
And feem'd bewilder'd with extatic joy;
Then fudden gloom her countenance deprefs'd,
Tears roll'd apace, and forrow heav'd her breaft;
Now calm again fhe filent view'd around   415
The proftrate Croud bent humbly to the ground:
Then caught with fudden rage fhe hurl'd about
Her thund'ring Anathema 'mong the Rout.

An aged wrinkl'd *Hag* the next appear'd,
Four mould'ring turrets o'er her temples rear'd;   420
In rows like beads the faithful medals tied,
In ornamental Ruft adorn'd her fide.
A broken Column of an ancient date
She dragg'd, and finking feem'd beneath the weight.
The Column all admir'd, the medals more,   425
" Th' Infcription value, but the Ruft adore."

The

The next to her approach'd a rev'rent *Dame,*
In trophies great from Infects torn fhe came ;
With ftately ftep fhe trod the plain along,
And threw her treafure 'midft th' admiring throng.   430
Forward with joy each curious Mortal fprang,
This caught a gaudy wing, and that a pointed fang.

Before the giddy throng, which now advanc'd,
With mincing ftep gay *Affectation* danc'd,
Then fudden ftop'd, and ftaring on the Croud   435
She frown'd, then fmil'd, and giggl'd out aloud.
The num'rous Throng attending round the Fair,
Mimick'd her geftures, and affum'd her air.

A croud of Mortals here with wond'ring eyes,
All pale and trembling gaz'd upon the fkies ;   440
Where on blue plains oppofing hofts engage,
While fhouts are heard and all the battle's rage.
Amidft the throng ftood cold and heartlefs *Fear,*
The fall of Nations whifp'ring in each ear.

Here pallid Spectres gleam'd, and there were feen   445
The Fairy Train in gambols on the green.
Through miry ways the ruftic journeys round,
Nor dares prefuming tread the hallow'd ground ;
Dire ills await the Wretch, fo fable fings,
Or pinch'd all o'er, or pierc'd with thoufand ftings.   450

The

The Structure ent'ring, as around I threw
My wond'ring eyes, gay forms arose to view.
False *Pleasure* here the borrow'd form of Joy
Assum'd, and roll'd around her sparkling eye.
But who, allur'd by her enchanting song,   455
From Virtue shrinks, and mingles with her throng,
Soon sees her beauties fade, and to his eyes
Deformity and sad Disease arise.

In a dark corner hell-born *Jealousy*
A wan and haggard Spright, I did espy;   460
Watchful she roll'd her ghastly eyes around,
And cautious trod to catch the whisp'ring sound.
Her heart forever deathless vultures tear,
And by her side stalk anguish and despair.
Curst is the wretch with her dire rage possess'd,   465
When fancy'd ills destroy his wonted rest.

Pale *Avarice* was seen with looks of care,
And clasp'd her bags with never-ceasing fear.
Close foll'wing her a wretched spectre came,
With tatter'd garments, *Poverty* her name,   470
In vain her search t'elude still *Avarice* strives,
Amidst her store in endless want she lives.

False *Honor* here I saw all gayly drest,
Glass were her beads, and tinsel'd was her vest;
Form'd in barbaric ages, rude her mien,   475
And in her hand the sanguin'd Sword was seen.

Not

Not ſtain'd like Patriots in their Country's cauſe,
To ſave Religion, or ſupport the Laws ;
In private Strife the crimſon torrents flow,
Their Country wounded by each fatal blow.   480

    With chequer'd hood *Diſſembling* ſtood behind,
And *Falſhood* coining lies to cheat Mankind ;
While with ſmooth art deceitful *Flattery*
Addreſs'd the ear of liſt'ning *Vanity*.

    The gloom was now diſclos'd where *Spleen* remain'd,   485
A thouſand various ills the Goddeſs pain'd.
As pow'rful Fancy works here Mortals are
Transform'd to glaſs, or China's brittle ware ;
Oppreſs'd by *Spleen* no longer joy they know,
For ever tortur'd with imagin'd woe.   490

    As thus I onward mov'd with wand'ring pace,
And view'd the varied wonders of the place ;
Juſt heav'n, I cry'd, Oh! give me to reſtrain
Imagination with a ſteady rein !
Tho' oft ſhe leads thro' *Pleaſure's* flow'ry ways,   495
In *Error's* thorny path ſhe ſometimes ſtrays.
Let me my hours with ſolid Judgment ſpend,
Nor to Deluſion's airy dreams attend ;
By *Reaſon* guided we ſhall only know
Thoſe heav'nly joys which *Fancy* can beſtow!   500

VICTORY.

VICTORY.

A POEM.

I.

O N a foft bank, wrapt in the gloomy groves,
 (Thro' which *Ohio's* ever rolling wave,
Unaw'd by moons, meandring wildly roves,
 And fweetly murm'ring feems to mourn the *brave ;*)

II.

Britannia fad reclin'd, and o'er *their* Grave
 Surcharg'd with grief her azure eyes did move,
Her plaint was aided by the mournful wave,
 And Zephyr to return her figh ftill ftrove.

III.

Her fpear and laurel-wreath afide were thrown,
 The big round pearly drops each other trace
From her bright eyes in gufhing torrents down,
 And wafh'd the rofes from her beauteous face.

IV.

" Ah! why, (then cry'd the bright angelic Maid)
 " Why is my breaft a prey to foul defpair ?
" It is but folly thus to mourn the *dead,*
 " No longer then I'll idly loiter here.

I   V. I'll

V.

" I'll feek where VICTORY her feat doth rear,
  " And all around her pow'rful influence fpread,
" She yet perhaps may liften to my pray'r,
  " And grant revenge for ev'ry gallant Shade."

VI.

Then fpread her fnowy wings, and fought the fkies,
  A lucent path proclaim'd the Goddefs' flight;
So thro' the air the ftreaming lightning flies,
  And leaves behind a dreadful blaze of light.

VII.

Above where Morning decks the lovely Eaft
  With the deep beauties of the Virgin's glow,
On her bright way *Britannia* fwiftly preft,
  And left the bufy worlds to roll below.

VIII.

And foon fhe gain'd the vaft amazing height,
  And foon the fhining Palace fhe efpies,
The maffy Gates wide op'ning, gave the bright
  Celeftial Beauty to her wond'ring eyes.

IX.

Rude was the Structures front, and round was heard
  The groans of anguifh echoing thro' the gloom,
Within bright majefty and grace appear'd,
  And founds of triumph fhook the fpacious Dome.

X. *Horror*

X.

Horror was Porter, with a ghaſtly ſtare
  His eye-brows rais'd, his mouth was open'd wide,
A hideous Concave! but no tongue was there,
  For ſpeech to him the angry Pow'rs deny'd.

XI.

The next grim *Death* was plac'd, and by his ſide
  Pale ſhiv'ring *Fear*, and ever writhing *Pain*,
His Siſter that, and this his gloomy Bride,
  Hung on his hand a dreadful helliſh Train.

XII.

Clad in deep ſables *Sorrow* did appear,
  All wan and ghaſtly with dejected eye,
Eager ſhe treaſur'd ev'ry Widow's tear,
  And number'd ev'ry helpleſs Orphan's ſigh.

XIII.

High on her ſhining ſeat was *Victory* plac'd,
  Sweet were her ſmiles, but dreadful was her frown,
Her left hand with the ſpreading palm was grac'd,
  And in her right ſhe held the Victor's crown.

XIV

One perfect Ruby was her glitt'ring throne,
  Gold were th' aſcending ſteps, but ſmear'd with blood,
Cloſe by her ſide bright laurel'd *Glory* ſhone,
  And *Fame* with her loud ſounding Trumpet ſtood.

I 2

XV.

XV.

Slav'ry, faft bound to her triumphant car,
   In anguifh gnafh'd her teeth, and fhook her chain,
While *Liberty* aloft, pois'd in the air,
   With pitying eye beheld the Mifcreant's pain.

XVI.

Behind brifk *Jollity*, in frolick mood,
   With the full Bowl, and crown'd with grapes, was fhown,
The Mufe, e'er grateful to the brave and good,
   Struck the foft Lyre with fweetnefs all her own.

XVII.

And now, the laft of all this varied throng,
   Sweet *Peace* was by her branching Olive known,
Smiling, with eafy fteps fhe fwept along,
   Nor e'er deform'd her beauties with a frown.

XVIII.

Around the wall, in curious niches plac'd,
   The imag'd Heroes fternly frown'd in gold,
Each warlike arm a polifh'd Falchin grac'd,
   Their brows were honor'd with the Laurel's fold.

XIX.

Or thofe who grac'd the happier days of old,
   Who to the heav'ns their envied names had rais'd,
Or thofe whom later ages had enroll'd,
   On the bright lift in fhining armour blaz'd.

XX.

XX.

Pruſſia, great Monarch! whom no fate can move,
  Superior 'bove the glorious Train appear'd,
In all the terrors of another Jove,
  While the dread bolt his ſable Eagle rear'd.

XXI.

Next *Ferdinand* ; who calm the War ſurveys,
  Serenity e'er gilds his princely breaſt,
So Neptune ſkims along the troubl'd waves,
  And ſmiling bids old Ocean be at reſt.

XXII.

O'er the bright pavement now, with eager haſte,
  (To where great *Victory* triumphant ſhone,
Rais'd on her glitt'ring ſeat) *Britannia* preſt,
  And humbly bow'd before her awful throne.

XXIII.

Then thus ſhe ſpoke, (but 'ere ſhe ſpeech could gain,
  She dropt freſh tears, and heav'd ſome poignant ſighs)
" Oh! brighteſt thou of the celeſtial train,
  " Ador'd by Man, and fav'rite of the Skies !

XXIV.

" Once was I bleſt, when o'er my infant days
  " Well pleas'd you ſmil'd, and rear'd me up to fame,
" Then did I wanton in thy glorious blaze,
  " And diſtant Nations trembl'd at my name !

XXV.

XXV.

" Then to my fway was Gallia forc'd to yield,
  " In vain fhe call'd her num'rous armies forth;
" Creffy and *Poitiers*, and the glorious field
  " Of *Agincourt*, proclaim'd my Britons worth.

XXVI.

" But now in vain, forfook by heav'n and Thee,
  " In vain they ftrive, their courage all is vain;
" Tho' the dear prize is Fame and Liberty,
  " They fee triumphant Slaves, and dread the chain.

XXVII.

" For pity (thou, who with a Mother's care,
  " Hung o'er my youth) propitious lend thy aid;
" Their baleful heads, fee the pale Lilies rear,
  " While my lov'd Rofes mourning droop and fade! "

XXVIII.

She ceas'd, nor could fhe more, diftreffing woe
  Her utt'rance ftopt, and cut the moving Tale,
Down her pale cheeks the briny torrents flow,
  Nor Hope could o'er her ftrength'ning Fears prevail.

XXIX.

Then *Vict'ry* thus, " Oh! thou, my Joy and Pride!
  " Near to my heart, and fav'rite of my train,
" Thou wouldft not thus have mourn'd had heav'n comply'd,
  " Nor had thy gallant Britons toil'd in vain.

XXX.

XXX.

" But now new laurels wait to grace thy brow,
 " And heav'n appeas'd, a chearing ray shall give,
" Thy glory then another dawn shall know,
 " Thy pow'r again, and all thy joys revive.

XXXI.

" Thy Fleets, the lordly Sovereigns of the Sea,
 " Shall bear from thee the terrors of the war,
" While Gallia pale, and trembling with dismay,
 " Shall shrink to view thy Navy from afar.

XXXII.

" Soon *Canada* shall own thy pow'rful sway,
 " Yet bleeding Conquest here will ask the tear,
" Like noble *Decius*, thy brave * Chief must pay
 " His life a victim for his Country here."

XXXIII.

She said, and while *Britannia* humbly bow'd,
 Bid willing Fame her silver trumpet sound,
Britannia's name rung thro' the vaults aloud,
 And Echo gave it to the heav'ns around !

---

 * General WOLFE.

A PARAPHRASE on the first PSALM.

1.

BLEST is the man who never lent
  To bold defigning men his ear,
Who, on his Country's good intent,
  From bribing Offices is clear:

2.

But ever conftant will remain
  Supporter of her lawful right,
Will firm her liberty maintain,
  Againft Oppreffors day and night.

3.

Like a fair Tree he fhall appear ;
  Which planted by fome River's fide,
Its fruit does in due feafon bear,
  And blooms in vernal Nature's pride.

4.

Thus fhall it flourifh, thus fhall rife,
  Its verdant Leaf fhall never fade,
Its beauties ftill fhall glad our eyes,
  And Pleafure dwell beneath its fhade.

5.

But men of dark bafe treachery,
  Like chaff before the active wind,
By giddy factions toft fhall be,
  Till left the fcorn of all Mankind.

6. Where

6.

Where Juſtice reigns they ſhun the place,
  Or where the open way doth ſhine,
Or where bright Truth our Senates grace,
  But veil'd by night they then deſign.

7.

To all the virtuous Patriot known,
  Shall ever live in endleſs fame,
Whilſt they (their deep laid ſchemes o'erthrown),
  Shall die, and with them die their name.

A CANTATA, on PEACE. 1763.
To Mr. N. E.

RECITATIVE.

WHERE *Schuylkil's* banks the ſhades adorn,
    And roſes op'ning to the morn,
      Give odours to the breeze;
Thus *Corydon*, a tuneful Swain,
Tun'd his ſoft reed a ſoothing ſtrain,
      By Nature form'd to pleaſe.
While Wood-Nymphs liſt'ning round him ſtood,
The Naiads left the oozy flood,
      Caught by the heav'nly ſong.
Attention, to the Muſe's aid,
Call'd *Silence* from her ſecret ſhade,
      And *Rapture* join'd the throng.

K   A I R.

AIR.

Let Pleafure fmile upon the plain,
 See *Peace*, with balmy wing,
Now hither bends her flight again,
 To crown the joyful fpring.

Clofe by the fair One's fide are feen,
 The *Arts*, with garlands dreft,
Gay *Commerce*, with engaging mien,
 And *Wealth*, with gaudy veft.

Now may the *Mufe* enjoy the fhade,
 Now tune her pleafing fong,
While wanton *Echo* thro' the glade
 Shall waft the ftrain along.

Then let all join the chearful found,
 'Tis *Peace*, fweet *Peace* we fing!
And let the joyful groves around
 With the loud *Chorus* ring.

CHORUS.

Then let all join the chearful found,
 'Tis *Peace*, fweet *Peace* we fing!
And let the joyful groves around
 With the loud *Chorus* ring.

SONGS.

SONGS.

I.

1.

THE day was clos'd beneath the ſhade,
  As penſive Celia ſat,
For Damon mourn'd the lovely Maid,
  And rail'd at envious fate.
Thus to the night ſhe gave her woe,
  While huſh'd was all the wood,
Still were the winds, the ſtreams ran ſlow,
  And *Silence* liſt'ning ſtood.

2.

Ah! but in vain are tears and ſighs,
  In vain muſt Celia mourn,
From me the faithleſs Damon flies,
  And leaves me but his ſcorn.
Why do the flatt'ring Shepherds ſay,
  Who ſees my beauty dies?
Why rob the Sovereign of the Day,
  To deck thoſe dreaded eyes?

K 2

3. Nor

3.

Nor are thofe arts to man confin'd,
  The limpid ftreams deceive,
In the foft mirror charms I find,
  And what I wifh believe.
But what are all thefe boafted charms;
  They cannot Damon move?
For glory now he leaves my arms,
  And flights my proffer'd love.

II.

1.

WHEN in *Celia's* heav'nly Eye
      Soft inviting Love I fpy,
Tho' you fay 'tis all a cheat,
I muft clafp the dear deceit.

2.

Why fhould I more knowledge gain,
When it only gives me pain?
If deceiv'd I'm ftill at reft,
In the fweet Delufion bleft.

III. To

III.

To S Y L V I A.

1.

WHY feek you to know what your fond *Damon* feels,
    Yet meet with derifion what Paffion reveals ?
Thy bofom proud *Sylvia* diftrefs ne'er could move,
Nor ever could feel the foft raptures of Love.

2.

When *Damon* would urge you with fighs, and with tears,
To pity his fuff'rings, you laugh at his fears ;
Thus cold, and thus cruel, thofe joys you'll ne'er find
Which virtue yields virtue in fympathy join'd.

3.

So fome curious Image whofe figure at moft,
And beautiful outfide is all it can boaft,
By the Artift's kind hand all its beauties are dreft,
And tho' mimicking Life is a Stone at the beft.

4.

Then hear me, proud *Sylvia*, nor boaft your bright charms,
Which ev'ry fond bofom fo pow'rfully warms,
While thus like an image of life, but a fhow,
You're fway'd by no Paffion, no Pleafure you'll know.

5. Accept

5.

Accept the advice which I friendly would give,
Drive hence Affectation e'er wrinkles arrive;
Or like fome maim'd ftatue, difdainful thrown by,
With rubbifh and lumber unheeded you'll lie.

IV.

1.

YOUNG *Thyrfis* with fighs often tells me his Tale,
    And artfully ftrives o'er my heart to prevail,
He fings me love-fongs as we trace thro' the Grove,
And on each fair Poplar hangs fonnets of love.
Tho' I often fmile on him to foften his pain,
(For wit I would have to embellifh my train)
I ftill put him off, for I have him fo faft,
I know he with joy will accept me at laft.

2.

Among the gay Tirbe that ftill flatter my pride,
There's *Cloddy* is handfome, and wealthy befide;
With fuch a gay partner more joys I can prove
Than to live in a Cottage with *Thyrfis* on love.
Tho' the Shepherd is gentle, yet blame me who can,
Since wealth, and not manners, 'tis now makes the man.
But fhould I fail here, and my hopes be all paft,
Fond *Thyrfis* I know will accept me at laft.

3.

Thus *Delia* enliven'd the grove with her ſtrain,
When *Thyrſis*, the Shepherd, came over the plain;
Bright *Chloris* he led, whom he'd juſt made his bride,
Joy ſhone in their eyes, as they walk'd ſide by ſide;
She ſcorn'd each low cunning, nor wiſh'd to deceive,
But all her delight was ſweet pleaſure to give.
In wedlock ſhe choſe to tye the Swain faſt,
For Shepherds will change if put off to the laſt.

V.

1.

O Come to * *Maſonborough's* grove,
  Ye Nymphs and Swains away,
Where blooming Innocence and Love,
  And Pleaſure crown the day.

2.

Here dwells the Muſe, here her bright Seat
  Erects the lovely Maid,
From Noiſe and Show, a bleſt retreat,
  She ſeeks the ſylvan ſhade.

3.

Hence Myra, with that ſcornful air,
  Nor frown within this grove,
Fell hate ſhall find no reſting here,
  'Tis ſacred all to Love.

---

* A pleaſant Retreat, nigh Cape Fear, in North-Carolina.

4, And

4.

And Chloe, on whofe wanton breaſt
　　Lafcivious breezes play,
'Tis Innocence that makes us bleſt,
　　And as the Seafon gay.

5.

Ye noiſy Revellers retire,
　　Bear your loud laughter hence,
'Tis Virtue fhall our fongs infpire,
　　And Mirth without offence.

6.

The Queen of Beauty, all divine,
　　Here fpreads her gentle reign,
See, all around, the graces fhine,
　　Like Cynthia's filver train.

VI.

1.

FOR *Chloris* long I figh'd in vain,
　　Nor could her bofom move,
She met my vows with cold difdain,
　　And fcorn return'd for Love.
At length, grown weary of her pride,
　　I left the haughty Maid,
Corinna's fetters now I try'd,
　　Who love for love repaid.

With

2.

With her the pleafing hours I wafte,
  With her fuch joys I prove,
As kindred Souls alone can tafte,
  When join'd in mutual Love.
Ye Shepherds here, nor flight my ftrain,
  Fly, fly the fcornful Fair,
Kind Nymphs you 'll find to eafe your pain,
  And foften ev'ry care.

VII.

AMYNTOR.

RECITATIVE.

LONG had *Amyntor* free from Love remain'd,
  The God enrag'd to fee his pow'r difdain'd,
Bent his beft bow, and aiming at his breaft
The fatal fhaft, he thus the Swain addreft.

AIR.

Hear me, hear me fenfelefs Rover,
Soon thou now fhallt be a Lover,
    Cupid will his pow'r maintain;
Haughty *Delia* fhall enflave thee,
Thou who thus infulting brav'ft me,
    Shalt unpity'd drag the chain.

L

RECITATIVE.

RECITATIVE.

He ceas'd, and quick he fhot the pointed dart,
Far fhort it fell, nor reach'd *Amyntor's* heart;
The angry God was fill'd with vaft furprize,
Abafh'd he ftood, while thus the Swain replies.

AIR.

Think not, Cupid, vain Deceiver,
I will own thy power ever,
  Guarded from thy' arts by Wine;
Haughty Beauty ne'er fhall grieve me,
Bacchus ftill fhall e'er relieve me,
  All his rofy joys are mine;
  All his rofy joys are mine.

THE

THE

ASSEMBLY of BIRDS;

from CHAUCER.

Begins at the thirteenth Stanza of Chaucer's Poem, called, "The Affembly of Fowles." The Argument of which is, all Fowles are gathered before Nature on St. Valentine's Day, to chufe their Mates. A Female Eagle being beloved of three Falcons, requireth a Year's refpite to make her Choice: Upon this Trial, *Qui bien aime tard oublie:* He that loveth well, is flow to forget.

Qui bien aime tard oublie.

TO weftern climes retir'd declining day,
  And night excluded ev'ry lucent ray;
In dens the wearied Beafts were couch'd to reft,
And each gay Warbler funk into her neft.
Sad *Philomel* alone, with plaintive ftrain,   5
Chac'd filence from Old Night's deep gloomy reign:
When lock'd in gentle flumber was I laid,
And, all around me, airy Phantoms play'd.
O *Cytherea!* love's all-pow'rful Queen,
'Twas thou who rais'd the beauteous mimic fcene.   10
Give me to know the facred fire again,
'Twas Love infpir'd, and Love fhall guide the pen.

L 2   The

The Sportfman fleeping on the dewy ground,
Purfues the Game, and chears the eager hound:
The Mifer tells in dreams his hidden ftore, 15
And warlike Knights fight all their battles o'er;
While thofe who burn amid the fever's rage,
In fancied Cups their parching thirft affwage.
Nor wonder then if I in dreams fhould ftray,
Where Love inviting makes the fiction gay. 20

In a wide plain methought that I was plac'd,
With Spring's gay liv'ry all the fcene was grac'd.
A lofty beauteous wall before me fhone,
Like em'rald green was ev'ry polifh'd ftone;
High in the front a maffy gate was rear'd, 25
Infcriptions on each glitt'ring fold appear'd.
Of gold and azure were the letters wrought,
But diff'rent feem'd to be the Writer's thought.

To that delightful place thro' ' me men go,
Where wounded hearts no longer feel their woe; 30
To that delightful place where ever gay,
And jocund, fports the green and lufty May.
No more let pining grief your breafts annoy,
Hafte, enter in, and tafte of deathlefs joy.

To that curs'd place, then fpake the other fide, 35
Men go thro' me where joy fhall ne'er abide;

To

To that curs'd place where trees no leaves ſhall bear,
But chilly Winter ſhivers thro' the year.
Here waſting Sorrow ſpreads her gloomy reign,
Danger attends, and ſad diſtreſsful Pain.   40
The varying ſcene aſtoniſh'd to behold,
A while I ſtood, ſometimes with fear made cold,
With warmer wiſhes then again grown bold.
In vain the Riddle to explain I try,
Still loath to enter, and as loath to fly.   45
So when the ever-faithful Needle ſet,
Between two Magnets, each of equal weight,
While pow'r to pow'er oppoſs'd, the war maintains,
Fix'd and immoveable it ſtill remains.

    As thus I ſtood, in thoughtful mood profound,   50
Soft melody ſeem'd floating all around.
The gates flew open-wide, new beauties riſe,
Gay pleaſing proſpects ſtruck my wond'ring eyes,
Fair ſpreading trees adorn'd the pleaſing ſcene,
By bounteous Nature dreſt all gay and green.   55
The builder Oak, the lofty pillar Elm,
The hardy Aſh, and the victorious Palm;
The Cypreſs, friend to Sorrow, mournful Tree,
The Fir, bold ſailor o'er the reſtleſs ſea.
The Holme for whipper's laſh, the Box tree too,   60
The Aſp for ſhafts, for bows the bending Yew;
The peaceful Olive, and the drunken Vine,
And Laurel ſacred to the tuneful Nine.

                                                    While

While round were feen the Hart, the Buck, the Hind,
The bounding Roe, and Beafts of ev'ry kind.   65

A garden faw I, full of pleafant bow'rs,
Clofe by a river's brink, enrich'd with flow'rs.
The curling ftreams in gentle murmurs glide,
And finny Squadrons fported down the tide.
While beauteous Swans in milk-white plumage dreft,   70
Againft the waves their downy bofoms preft.
On ev'ry bough the Birds were hear'd to fing,
As when they joyous hail the gladfome Spring.
And gentle Zephyr foftly whifp'ring round,
Seem'd join'd accordant to the pleafing found.   75
Mild was the air, the fky ferene and clear,
And fpring eternal crown'd the rolling year.
Here wan Difeafe was never known to tread,
Nor palfy age to fhake his hoary head:
Health painted rofy blufhes on each face,   80
And blooming youth gave ev'ry other grace.
Here day for ever fhone, no night was here,
But light and joy ftill banifh'd ev'ry fear.

Enticing Pleafure there I did efpy,
Sweet were her looks, and full of courtefy.   85
Beneath a fpreading oak there as I guefs,
Saw I Delight, and with him Gentlenefs.
There faw I Beauty, in a nice attire,
And Youth, with Jollity and warm Defire.

Falfe

Falfe Flatt'ry, Favour, Diligence, and Three   90
Whofe names fhall not be here difclos'd by me.

On lofty jafper Pillars rais'd on high,
A Temple 'rofe, and feem'd to kifs the fky.
Here Nymphs for ever danc'd an endlefs round,
A varied Train, fome with fad myrtle crown'd,   95
Their garments torn, with loofe difhevel'd hair,
And on their brows was forrow mark'd, and care.
Others more gay, in flow'ry garlands dreft,
And Joy and Gladnefs feem'd to fwell each breaft.
With looks ferene, clofe by the Structure's gate;   100
Peace with her lovely blooming Olives fat.
Sweet was her envied fmile, and by her fide,
Pale Patience, on a fandy bank, I fpy'd.
Here Art was feated, with her fhining train,
And Majefty fpread round her high domain.   105

On the bright Roof with gold and azure grac'd,
Full many thoufand pair of Doves were plac'd.
Gay Wealth ftood Porter at the Temple door,
And in his hand a golden wand he bore.
At whofe all pow'rful touch the Gates remove,   110
And open all the fhining Courts of Love.
Haughty his mien, Pride fat upon his brow!
And loofely down his glitt'ring veftments flow.
Ent'ring within I heard unnumber'd fighs,
Such as from fond defpairing Lovers rife;   115

Warm

Warm was the Gale, and kindl'd by Defire,
And ev'ry Breaft feem'd fcorch'd with inward fire.

On a rich bed bright fea-born *Venus* laid,
Her loofe thin veftments ev'ry charm betray'd;
In golden fillets were her treffes bound,   120
The blooming Graces all were waiting round.
Fair bounteous *Ceres* by the Goddefs ftood,
And youthful *Bacchus*, in a frolic mood.
His brows were with bright purple honors dreft,
While in the Bowl the juicy grape he preft.   125
,Tis fprightly Wine can the dull paffions move,
And *Ceres'* bleffings give us pow'r to Love.

High on a fhining feat with rubies grac'd,
Cupid, the God of am'rous thoughts, was plac'd.
Bent was his bow, and in his hand a dart   130
He held, on which was fixt a bleeding heart;
Around his throne unnumber'd crouds attend,
And to the God in awful rev'rence bend.
Their pray'rs with mingl'd fighs they loud prefer'd,
Like rolling thunder from a diftance heard.   135

Around, as trophies, bows were caft unftrung,
And ufelefs now, the empty quivers hung.
Once by bright Nymphs thefe fhining arms were borne,
Who ftrict to keep *Diana's* law had fworn.

In

In vain the Goddefs call'd, the defert Grove   140
They left, and fped to tafte the fweets of Love.
The fhining wall with tales was painted o'er,
Of thofe who bow'd to Love's almighty pow'r.

In a fair Grove, which near the Temple ftood,
Thro' which there gently roll'd a murm'ring flood;   145
Rais'd on a bank, with fragrant flow'rs made gay,
Great NATURE fat, whofe laws we all obey.
(As Summer's fun the Stars in light excel,
So fhe furpaffes all that tongue can tell.)
Around the Dame the Birds affembl'd all,   150
For 'twas *St. Valentine's* great feftival.
Each to felect his mate did now appear,
So ancient cuftom fix'd from year to year.

The higheft feats the Birds of prey did grace,
Who fed on worms enjoy'd the fecond place;   155
While thofe who humbler fed on feeds were feen,
Unnumber'd fpread along th' enamel'd green.

And here might men the royal Eagle find,
With other Eagles of a lower kind;
The gentle Falcon, and the Popinjay,   160
And Peacock in his angel-feathers gay;
The jealous Swan, the fcornful Jay and Stare,
The boding Owl, and Crow with voice of care;

M   The

The Chough to thiev'ry prone, the chatt'ring Pye,
And the falfe Lapwing full of treachery.　　　　　165
The Sparrow, Venus' fon, the Nightingale,
And Swallow, Murtherer of the bees fo fmall;
The Pheafant, Scorner of the Cock by night,
With the tame Ruddock, and the coward Kite.
The Cuckoo ftill unkind, the Crane, the Geaunt,　　170
The wakeful Goofe, and glutton Cormorant;
The wedded Turtle, and the Goofehawke rare,
The Throftle old, and the frofty Fieldefare.
With numbers more, whofe names I fhall not tell,
Who in fhrill notes, or gaudy drefs excel.　　　　175

———*Left unfinifhed* ———

THE

THE

PRINCE of PARTHIA,

A TRAGEDY.

M 2

Dramatis Perſonæ.

MEN.

Artabanus, King of Parthia.

Arſaces, ⎫
Vardanes, ⎬ his Sons.
Gotarzes, ⎭

Barzaphernes, Lieutenant-General, under Arſaces.

Lyſias, ⎫
Phraates, ⎬ Officers at Court.

Bethas, a Nöble Captive.

WOMEN.

Thermuſa, the Queen.

Evanthe, belov'd by Arſaces.

Cleone, her Confident.

Edeſſa, Attendant on the Queen.

Guards and Attendants.

Scene, CTESIPHON.

Advertisement.

OUR Author has made Use of the *licentia poetica* in the Management of this Dramatic Piece; and deviates, in a particular or two, from what is agreed on by Historians : The Queen *Thermusa* being not the Wife of King *Artabanus*, but (according to *Tacitus, Strabo* and *Josephus*) of *Phraates*; *Artabanus* being the fourth King of *Parthia* after him. Such Lapses are not unprecedented among the Poets; and will the more readily admit of an Excuse, when the Voice of History is followed in the Description of Characters.

The PRINCE of PARTHIA,

A TRAGEDY.

ACT I. SCENE I.

The Temple of the SUN.

GOTARZES and PHRAATES.

GOTARZES.

HE comes, *Arſaces* comes, my gallant Brother
(Like ſhining Mars in all the pomp of conqueſt)
Triumphant enters now our joyful gates;
Bright Victory waits on his glitt'ring car,
And ſhows her fav'rite to the wond'ring croud;
While Fame exulting ſounds the happy name
To realms remote, and bids the world admire.
Oh! 'tis a glorious day:——let none preſume
T' indulge the tear, or wear the gloom of ſorrow;
This day ſhall ſhine in Ages yet to come,
And grace the PARTHIAN ſtory.

PHRAATES.

PHRAATES.

Glad *Ctes'phon*
Pours forth her numbers, like a rolling deluge,
To meet the blooming Hero; all the ways,
On either fide, as far as fight can ftretch,
Are lin'd with crouds, and on the lofty walls
Innumerable multitudes are rang'd.
On ev'ry countenance impatience fate
With roving eye, before the train appear'd.
But when they faw the Darling of the Fates,
They rent the air with loud repeated fhouts;
The Mother fhow'd him to her infant Son,
And taught his lifping tongue to name *Arfaces*:
E'en aged Sires, whofe founds are fcarcely heard,
By feeble ftrength fupported, toft their caps,
And gave their murmur to the gen'ral voice.

GOTARZES.

The fpacious ftreets, which lead up to the Temple,
Are ftrew'd with flow'rs; each, with frantic joy,
His garland forms, and throws it in the way.
What pleafure, *Phraates*, muft fwell his bofom,
So fee the proftrate nation all around him,
And know he's made them happy! to hear them
Teafe the Gods, to fhow'r their bleffings on him!
Happy *Arfaces*! fain I'd imitate
Thy matchlefs worth, and be a fhining joy!

PHRAATES.

PHRAATES

Hark! what a fhout was that which pierc'd the fkies!
It feem'd as tho' all Nature's beings join'd,
To hail thy glorious Brother.

GOTARZES.

Happy *Parthia!*
Now proud *Arabia* dreads her deftin'd chains,
While fhame and rout difperfes all her fons.
Barzaphernes purfues the fugitives,
The few whom fav'ring Night redeem'd from flaughter;
Swiftly they fled, for fear had wing'd their fpeed,
And made them blefs the fhade which faf'ty gave.

PHRAATES.

What a bright hope is ours, when thofe dread pow'rs
Who rule yon heav'n, and guide the mov'ments here,
Shall call your royal Father to their joys:
In bleft *Arfaces* ev'ry virtue meets;
He's gen'rous, brave, and wife, and good,
Has fkill to act, and noble fortitude
To face bold danger, in the battle firm,
And dauntlefs as a Lion fronts his foe.
Yet is he fway'd by ev'ry tender paffion,
Forgiving mercy, gentlenefs and love;
Which fpeak the Hero friend of humankind.

N   GOTARZES.

GOTARZES.

'And let me fpeak, for 'tis to him I owe
That here I ftand, and breath the common air,
And 'tis my pride to tell it to the world.
One lucklefs day as in the eager chace
My Courfer wildly bore me from the reft,
A monft'rous Leopard from a bofky fen
Rufh'd forth, and foaming lafh'd the ground,
And fiercely ey'd me as his deftin'd quarry.
My jav'lin fwift I threw, but o'er his head
It erring pafs'd, and harmlefs in the air
Spent all its force; my falchin then I feiz'd,
Advancing to attack my ireful foe,
When furioufly the favage fprung upon me,
And tore me to the ground; my treach'rous blade
Above my hand fnap'd fhort, and left me quite
Defencelefs to his rage; *Arfaces* then,
Hearing the din, flew like fome pitying pow'r,
And quickly freed me from the Monfter's paws,
Drenching his bright lance in his fpotted breaft.

PHRAATES.

How diff'rent he from arrogant *Vardanes?*
That haughty Prince eyes with a ftern contempt
All other Mortals, and with lofty mien
He treads the earth as tho' he were a God.
Nay, I believe that his ambitious foul,
Had it but pow'r to its licentious wifhes,

Would

Would dare difpute with Jove the rule of heav'n;
Like a Titanian fon with giant infolence,
Match with the Gods, and wage immortal war,
'Til their red wrath fhould hurl him headlong down,
E'en to deftruction's loweft pit of horror.

GOTARZES.

Methinks he wears not that becoming joy
Which on this bright occafion gilds the court;
His brow's contracted with a gloomy frown,
Penfive he ftalks along, and feems a prey
To pining difcontent.

PHRAATES.

Arfaces he diflikes,
For ftanding 'twixt him, and the hope of Empire;
While Envy, like a rav'nous Vulture tears
His canker'd heart, to fee your Brother's triumph.

GOTARZES.

And yet *Vardanes* owes that hated Brother
As much as I; 'twas fummer laft, as we
Were bathing in *Euphrates*' flood, *Vardanes*
Proud of ftrength would feek the further fhore;
But 'ere he the mid-ftream gain'd, a poignant pain
Shot thro' his well-ftrung nerves, contracting all,
And the ftiff joints refus'd their wonted aid.

Loudly

Loudly he cry'd for help, *Arſaces* heard,
And thro' the ſwelling waves he ruſh'd to ſave
His drowning Brother, and gave him life,
And for the boon the Ingrate pays him hate.

PHRAATES.

There's ſomething in the wind, for I've obſerv'd
Of late he much frequents the Queen's apartment,
And fain would court her favour, wild is ſhe
To gain revenge for fell *Vonones'* death,
And firm reſolves the ruin of *Arſaces*.
Becauſe that fill'd with filial piety,
To ſave his Royal Sire, he ſtruck the bold
Preſumptuous Traitor dead ; nor heeds ſhe
The hand which gave her Liberty, nay rais'd her
Again to Royalty.

GOTARZES.

Ingratitude,
Thou hell-born fiend, how horrid is thy form!
The Gods ſure let thee looſe to ſcourge mankind,
And ſave them from an endleſs waſte of thunder.

PHRAATES.

Yet I've beheld this now ſo haughty Queen,
Bent with diſtreſs, and e'en by pride forſook,
When following thy Sire's triumphant car,
Her tears and ravings mov'd the ſenſeleſs herd,

And

And pity bleſt their more than ſavage breaſts,
With the ſhort pleaſure of a moments ſoftneſs.
Thy Father, conquer'd by her charms, (for what
Can charm like mourning beauty) ſoon ſtruck off
Her chains, and rais'd her to his bed and throne.
Adorn'd the brows of her aſpiring Son,
The fierce *Vonones*, with the regal crown
Of rich *Armenia*, once the happy rule
Of *Tiſaphernes*, her deceaſed Lord.

GOTARZES.

And he in waſteful war return'd his thanks,
Refus'd the homage he had ſworn to pay,
And ſpread Deſtruction ev'ry where around,
'Til from *Arſaces* hand he met the fate
His crimes deſerv'd.

PHRAATES.

As yet your princely Brother
Has ſcap'd *Thermuſa's* rage, for ſtill reſiding
In peaceful times, within his Province, ne'er
Has fortune bleſt her with a ſight of him,
On whom ſhe'd wreck her vengeance.

GOTARZES.

She has won
By ſpells, I think, ſo much on my fond father,
That he is guided by her will alone.

She rules the realm, her pleasure is a law,
All offices and favours are bestow'd,
As she directs.

PHRAATES.

But see, the Prince, *Vardanes*,
Proud *Lysias* with him, he whose soul is harsh
With jarring discord. Nought but madding rage,
And ruffian-like revenge his breast can know,
Indeed to gain a point he'll condescend
To mask the native rancour of his heart,
And smooth his venom'd tongue with flattery.
Assiduous now he courts *Vardanes*' friendship,
See, how he seems to answer all his gloom,
And give him frown for frown.

GOTARZES.

Let us retire,
And shun them now; I know not what it means,
But chilling horror shivers o'er my limbs,
When *Lysias* I behold.——

SCENE

SCENE II.

VARDANES and LYSIAS.

LYSIAS.

That fhout proclaims   [Shout.
Arfaces near approach.

VARDANES.

Peace, prithee peace,
Wilt thou ftill fhock me with that hated found,
And grate harfh difcord in my offended ear?
If thou art fond of echoing the name,
Join with the fervile croud, and hail his triumph.

LYSIAS.

I hail him? By our glorious fhining God,
I'd fooner lofe my fpeech, and all my days
In filence reft, converfing with my thoughts,
Than hail *Arfaces.*

VARDANES.

Yet, again his name,
Sure there is magic in it, PARTHIA's drunk
And giddy with the joy; the houfes tops
With gaping fpectators are throng'd, nay wild
They climb fuch precipices that the eye
Is dazzl'd with their daring; ev'ry wretch

Who

Who long has been immur'd, nor dar'd enjoy
The common benefits of fun and air,
Creeps from his lurking place; e'en feeble age,
Long to the fickly couch confin'd, ftalks forth,
And with infectious breath affails the Gods.
O! curfe the name, the idol of their joy.

LYSIAS.

And what's that name, that thus they fhould difturb
The ambient air, and weary gracious heav'n
With ceafelefs bellowings? *Vardanes* founds
With equal harmony, and fuits as well
The loud repeated fhouts of noify joy.
Can he bid Chaos Nature's rule diffolve,
Can he deprive mankind of light and day,
And turn the Seafons from their deftin'd courfe?
Say, can he do all this, and be a God?
If not, what is his matchlefs merit? What dares he,
Vardanes dares not? blufh not noble prince,
For praife is merit's due, and I will give it;
E'en mid the croud which waits thy Brother's fmile,
I'd loud proclaim the merit of *Vardanes.*

VARDANES.

Forbear this warmth, your friendfhip urges far.
Yet know your love fhall e'er retain a place
In my remembrance. There is fomething here —   {pointing to
                                                 {his breaft.

Another

Another time and I will give thee all;
But now, no more.——

LYSIAS.

You may command my fervice,
I'm happy to obey. Of late your Brother
Delights in hind'ring my advancement, ..
And ev'ry boafter's rais'd above my merit,
Barzaphernes alone commands his ear,
His oracle in all.

VARDANES.

I hate *Arfaces*,
Tho' he's my Mother's fon, and churchmen fay
There's fomething facred in the name of Brother.
My foul endures him not, and he's the bane
Of all my hopes of greatnefs. Like the fun
He rules the day, and like the night's pale Queen,
My fainter beams are loft when he appears.
And this becaufe he came into the world,
A moon or two before me: What's the diff'rence,
That he alone fhould fhine in Empire's feat?
I am not apt to trumpet forth my praife,
Or highly name myfelf, but this I'll fpeak,
To him in ought, I'm not the leaft inferior.
Ambition, glorious fever! mark of Kings,
Gave me immortal thirft and rule of Empire.

O

Why

Why lag'd my tardy foul, why droop'd the wing,
Nor forward fpringing, fhot before his fpeed
To feize the prize?—'Twas Empire—Oh! 'twas Empire—

LYSIAS.

Yet, I muft think that of fuperior mould
Your foul was form'd, fit for a heav'nly ftate,
And left reluctant its fublime abode,
And painfully obey'd the dread command,
When Jove's controuling fate forc'd it below.
His foul was earthly, and it downward mov'd,
Swift as to the center of attraction.

VARDANES.

It might be fo——But I've another caufe
To hate this Brother, ev'ry way my rival;
In love as well as glory he's above me;
I dote on fair *Evanthe*, but the charmer
Difdains my ardent fuit, like a mifer
He treafures up her beauties to himfelf:
Thus is he form'd to give me torture ever.——
But hark, they've reach'd the Temple,
Didft thou obferve the croud, their eagernefs,
Each put the next afide to catch a look,
Himfelf was elbow'd out?——Curfe, curfe their zeal——

LYSIAS.

Stupid folly!

VARDANES.

VARDANES.

I'll tell thee *Lyfias*,
This many-headed monfter multitude,
Unfteady is as giddy fortune's wheel,
As woman fickle, varying as the wind;
To day they this way courfe, the'next they veer,
And fhift another point, the next another.

LYSIAS.

Curiofity's another name for man,
The blazing meteor ftreaming thro' the air
Commands our wonder, and admiring eyes,
With eager gaze we trace the lucent path,
'Til fpent at length it fhrinks to native nothing.
While the bright ftars which ever fteady glow,
Unheeded fhine, and blefs the world below.

SENE III.

QUEEN and EDESSA.

QUEEN.

Oh! give me way, the haughty victor comes,
Surrounded by adoring multitudes;
On fwelling tides of praife to heav'n they raife him;
To deck their idol, they rob the glorious beings
Of their fplendor.

O 2

EDESSA.

My royal Lady,
Chace hence thefe paffions.

QUEEN.

Peace, forever peace,
Have I not caufe to hate this homicide?
'Twas by his curfed hand *Vonones* fell,
Yet fell not as became his gallant fpirit,
Not by the warlike arm of chief renown'd,
But by a youth, ye Gods, a beardlefs ftripling,
Stab'd by his daftard falchin from behind;
For well I know he fear'd to meet *Vonones*,
As princely warriors meet with open daring,
But fhrunk amidft his guards, and gave him death,
When faint with wounds, and weary with the fight.

EDESSA.

With anguifh I have heard his haplefs fate,
And mourn'd in filence for the gallant Prince.

QUEEN.

Soft is thy nature, but alas! *Edeffa*,
Thy heart's a ftranger to a mother's forrows,
To fee the pride of all her wifhes blafted;
Thy fancy cannot paint the ftorm of grief,
Defpair and anguifh, which my breaft has known.

Oh!

Oh! show'r, ye Gods, your torments on *Arsaces*,
Curs'd be the morn which dawn'd upon his birth.

EDESSA.

Yet, I intreat———

QUEEN.

　　　　　Away! for I will curse———
O may he never know a father's fondness,
Or know it to his sorrow, may his hopes
Of joy be cut like mine, and his short life
Be one continu'd tempest; if he lives,
Let him be curs'd with jealousy and fear,
And vext with anguish of neglecting scorn;
May tort'ring hope present the flowing cup,
Then hasty snatch it from his eager thirst,
And when he dies base treach'ry be the means.

EDESSA.

Oh! calm your spirits.

QUEEN.

　　　　　Yes, I'll now be calm,
Calm as the sea when the rude waves are laid,
And nothing but a gentle swell remains;
My curse is heard, and I shall have revenge:
There's something here which tells me 'twill be so,
And peace resumes her empire o'er my breast.

Vardanes

Vardanes is the Minifter of Vengeance;
Fir'd by ambition, he afpiring feeks
T' adorn his brows with *Parthia's* diadem;
I 've fann'd the fire, and wrought him up to fury,
Envy fhall urge him forward ftill to dare,
And difcord be the prelude to deftruction,
Then this deteiled race fhall feel my hate.

EDESSA.

And doth thy hatred then extend fo far,
That innocent and guilty all alike
Muft feel thy dreadful vengeance?

QUEEN.

Ah! *Edeffa,*
Thou doft not know e'en half my mighty wrongs,
But in thy bofom I will pour my forrows.

EDESSA.

With fecrecy I ever have repaid
Your confidence.

QUEEN.

I know thou haft, then hear,
The changeling King who oft has kneel'd before me,
And own'd no other pow'r, now treats me
With ill diffembl'd love mix'd with difdain,
A newer beauty rules his faithlefs heart,

Which

Which only in variety is bleſt;
Oft have I heard him, when wrapt up in ſleep,
And wanton fancy rais'd the mimic ſcene,
Call with unuſual fondneſs on *Euanthe*;
While I have lain neglected by his ſide,
Except ſometimes in a miſtaken rapture
He'd claſp me to his boſom.

EDESSA.

Oh! Madam,
Let not corroding jealouſy uſurp
Your Royal breaſt, unnumber'd ills attend
The wretch who entertains that fatal gueſt.

QUEEN.

Think not that I'll purſue its wandring fires,
No more I'll know perplexing doubts and fears,
And erring trace ſuſpicion's endleſs maze,
For, ah! I doubt no more.

EDESSA.

Their ſhouts approach.

QUEEN.

Lead me, *Edeſſa*, to ſome peaceful gloom,
Some ſilent ſhade far from the walks of men,
There ſhall the hop'd revenge my thoughts employ,
And ſooth my ſorrows with the coming joy.

SCENE

SCENE IV.

EVANTHE and CLEONE.

EVANTHE.

No I'll not meet him now, for love delights
In the foft pleafures of the fecret fhade,
And fhuns the noife and tumult of the croud.
How tedious are the hours which bring him
To my fond panting heart! for oh! to thofe
Who live in expectation of the blifs,
Time flowly creeps, and ev'ry tardy minute
Seems mocking of their wifhes. Say, *Cleone*,
For you beheld the triumph, midft his pomp,
Did he not feem to curfe the empty fhow,
The pageant greatnefs, enemy to love,
Which held him from *Evanthe?* hafte, to tell me,
And feed my gready ear with the fond tale——
Yet, hold—for I fhall weary you with queftions,
And ne'er be fatisfied—Beware, *Cleone*,
And guard your heart from Love's delufive fweets.

CLEONE.

Is Love an ill, that thus you caution me
To fhun his pow'r?

EVANTHE.

EVANTHE.

The Tyrant, my *Cleone*,
Defpotic rules, and fetters all our thoughts.
Oh! wouldſt thou love, then bid adieu to peace,
Then fears will come, and jealouſies intrude,
Ravage your boſom, and diſturb your quiet,
E'en pleaſure to exceſs will be a pain.
Once I was free, then my exulting heart
Was like a bird that hops from ſpray to ſpray,
And all was innocence and mirth; but, lo!
The Fowler came, and by his arts decoy'd,
And ſoon the Wanton cag'd. Twice fifteen times
Has *Cynthia* dipt her horns in beams of light,
Twice fifteen times has waſted all her brightneſs,
Since firſt I knew to love; 'twas on that day
When curs'd *Vonones* fell upon the plain,
The lovely Victor doubly conquer'd me.

CLEONE.

Forgive my boldneſs, Madam, if I aſk
What chance firſt gave you to *Vonones*' pow'r?
Curioſity thou know'ſt is of our ſex.

EVANTHE.

That is a taſk will wake me to new ſorrows,
Yet thou attend, and I will tell thee all.
Arabia gave me birth, my father held
Great Offices at Court, and was reputed

P

Brave,

Brave, wife and loyal, by his Prince belov'd.
Oft has he led his conqu'ring troops, and forc'd
From frowning victory her awful honours.
In infancy I was his only treafure,
On me he wafted all his ftore of fondnefs.
Oh! I could tell thee of his wond'rous goodnefs,
His more than father's love and tendernefs.
But thou wouldft jeer, and fay the tale was trifling;
So did he dote upon me, for in childhood
My infant charms, and artlefs innocence
Bleft his fond age, and won on ev'ry heart.
But, oh! from this fprung ev'ry future ill,
This fatal beauty was the fource of all.

CLEONE.

'Tis often fo, for beauty is a flow'r
That tempts the hand to pluck it.

EVANTHE.

Full three times
Has fcorching fummer fled from cold winter's
Ruthlefs blafts, as oft again has fpring
In fprightly youth dreft nature in her beauties,
Since bathing in * Niphates' filver ftream,
Attended only by one fav'rite maid;
As we were fporting on the wanton waves,
Swift from the wood a troop of horfemen rufh'd,
Rudely they feiz'd, and bore me trembling off,

---

* The Tigris.

In

In vain *Edeſſa* with her ſhrieks aſſail'd
The heav'ns, for heav'n was deaf to both our pray'rs.
The wretch whoſe inſolent embrace confin'd me,
(Like thunder burſting on the guilty ſoul)
With curs'd *Vonones* voice pour'd in my ears
A hateful tale of love; for he it ſeems
Had ſeen me at Arabia's royal court,
And took thoſe means to force me to his arms.

CLEONE.

Perhaps you may gain ſomething from the Captives
Of your loſt Parents.

EVANTHE.

This I mean to try,
Soon as the night hides Nature in her darkneſs,
Veil'd in the gloom we'll ſteal into their priſon.
But, oh! perhaps e'en now my aged Sire
May 'mongſt the ſlain lie weltring on the field,
Pierc'd like a riddle through with num'rous wounds,
While parting life is quiv'ring on his lips,
He may perhaps be calling on his *Evanthe*.
Yes, ye great Pow'rs who boaſt the name of mercy,
Ye have deny'd me to his lateſt moments,
To all the offices of filial duty,
To bind his wounds, and waſh them with my tears,
Is this, is this your mercy?

P 2

CLEONE.

Blame not heav'n,
For heav'n is juft and kind; dear Lady drive
Thefe black ideas from your gentle breaft;
Fancy delights to torture the diftrefs'd,
And fill the gloomy fcene with fhadowy ills,
Summon your reafon, and you'll foon have comfort.

EVANTHE.

Doft thou name comfort to me, my *Cleone*,
Thou who know'ft all my forrows? plead no more,
'Tis reafon tells me I am doubly wretched.

CLEONE.

But hark, the mufic ftrikes, the rites begin,
And, fee, the doors are op'ning.

EVANTHE.

Let's retire;
My heart is now too full to meet him here,
Fly fwift ye hours, till in his arms I'm preft,
And each intruding care is hufh'd to reft.

SCENE

SCENE V.

The Scene draws and difcovers, in the inner Part of the Temple, a large
Image of the Sun, with an Altar before it. Around Priefts and
Attendants.

KING, ARSACES, VARDANES, GOTARZES, PHRAATES, LYSIAS,
with BETHAS in chains.

HYMN.

Parent of Light, to thee belong
Our grateful tributary fongs;
Each thankful voice to thee fhall rife,
And chearful pierce the azure fkies;
While in thy praife all earth combines,
And Echo in the Chorus joins.

All the gay pride of blooming May,
   The Lily fair and blufhing Rofe,
To thee their early honours pay,
   And all their heav'nly fweets difclofe.
The feather'd Choir on ev'ry tree
   To hail thy glorious dawn repair,
While the fweet fons of harmony
   With Hallelujah's fill the air.

'Tis

'Tis thou haſt brac'd the Hero's arm,
And giv'n the Love of praiſe to warm,
His boſom, as he onward flies,
And for his Country bravely dies.
Thine's victory, and from thee ſprings
Ambition's fire, which glows in Kings.

KING (coming forward.)

Thus, to the Gods our tributary ſongs,
And now, oh! let me welcome once again
My blooming victor to his Father's arms;
And let me thank thee for our ſafety: PARTHIA
Shall thank thee too, and give her grateful praiſe
To her Deliverer.

OMNES.

All hail! *Arſaces!*

KING.

Thanks to my loyal friends.

VARDANES.   [Aſide.

Curſe, curſe the ſound,
E'en Echo gives it back with int'reſt,
The joyful gales ſwell with the pleaſing theme,
And waft it far away to diſtant hills.
O that my breath was poiſon, then indeed
I'd hail him like the reſt, but blaſt him too.

ARSACES.

ARSACES.

My Royal Sire, thefe honours are unmerited,
Beneath your profp'rous aufpices I fought,
Bright vict'ry to your banners joyful flew,
And favour'd for the Sire the happy fon.
But lenity fhould grace the victor's laurels,
Then, here, my gracious Father——

KING.

Ha! 'tis *Bethas!*
Know'ft thou, vain wretch, what fate attends on thofe
Who dare oppofe the pow'r of mighty Kings,
Whom heav'n delights to favour? fure fome God
Who fought to punifh you for impious deeds,
'Twas urg'd you forward to infult our arms,
And brave us at our Royal City's gates.

BETHAS.

At honour's call, and at my King's command,
Tho' it were even with my fingle arm, again
I'd brave the multitude, which, like a deluge,
O'erwhelm'd my gallant handful; yea wou'd meet
Undaunted, all the fury of the torrent.
'Tis honour is the guide of all my actions,
The ruling ftar by which I fteer thro' life,
And fhun the fhelves of infamcy and vice.

KING.

KING.

It was the thirst of gain which drew you on;
'Tis thus that Av'rice always cloaks its views,
Th' ambition of your Prince you gladly snatch'd
As opportunity to fill your coffers.
It was the plunder of our palaces,
And of our wealthy cities, fill'd your dreams,
And urg'd you on your way; but you have met
The due reward of your audacity.
Now shake your chains, shake and delight your ears
With the soft music of your golden fetters.

BETHAS.

True, I am fall'n, but glorious was my fall,
The day was brav'ly fought, we did our best,
But victory's of heav'n. Look o'er yon field,
See if thou findest one *Arabian* back
Disfigur'd with dishonourable wounds.
No, here, deep on their bosoms, are engrav'd
The marks of honour! 'twas thro' here their souls
Flew to their blissful seats. Oh! why did I
Survive the fatal day? To be this slave,
To be the gaze and sport of vulgar crouds,
Thus like a shackl'd tyger stalk my round,
And grimly low'r upon the shouting herd.
Ye Gods!—

                                        KING.

KING.

Away with him to inftant death.

ARSACES.

Hear me, my Lord, O, not on this bright day,
Let not this day of joy blufh with his blood.
Nor count his fteady loyalty a crime,
But give him life, *Arfaces* humbly afks it,
And may you e'er be ferv'd with honeft hearts.

KING.

Well, be it fo; hence, bear him to his dungeon;
Lyfias, we here commit him to thy charge.

BETHAS.

Welcome my dungeon, but more welcome death.
Truft not too much, vain Monarch, to your pow'r,
Know fortune places all her choiceft gifts
On ticklifh heights, they fhake with ev'ry breeze,
And oft fome rude wind hurls them to the ground.
Jove's thunder ftrikes the lofty palaces,
While the low cottage, in humility,
Securely ftands, and fees the mighty ruin.
What King can boaft, to morrow as to day,
Thus, happy will I reign? The rifing fun
May view him feated on a fplendid throne,
And, fetting, fee him fhake the fervile chain.

[*Exit guarded.*

Q   SCENE

SCENE VI.

KING, ARSACES, VARDANES, GOTARZES, PHRAATES.

GOTARZES.

Thus let me hail thee from the croud diftinct,
For in the exulting voice of gen'ral joy
My fainter founds were loft, believe me, Brother,
My foul dilates with joy to fee thee thus.

ARSACES.

Thus let me thank thee in this fond embrace.

VARDANES.

The next will be my turn, Gods, I had rather
Be circl'd in a venom'd ferpent's fold.

GOTARZES.

O, my lov'd Brother, 'tis my humble boon,
That, when the war next calls you to the field,
I may attend you in the rage of battle.
By imitating thy heroic deeds,
Perhaps, I may rife to fome little worth,
Beneath thy care I'll try my feeble wings,
Till taught by thee to foar to nobler heights.

KING.

KING

Why that's my boy, thy fpirit fpeaks thy birth,
No more I'll turn thee from the road to glory,
To ruft in flothfulnefs, with lazy Gownfmen.

GOTARZES.

Thanks, to my Sire, I'm now completely bleft.

ARSACES.

But, I've another Brother, where's *Vardanes?*

KING.

Ha! what, methinks, he lurks behind the croud,
And wears a gloom which fuits not with the time.

VARDANES.

Doubt not my Love, tho' I lack eloquence,
To drefs my fentiments and catch the ear,
Tho' plain my manners, and my language rude,
My honeft heart difdains to wear difguife.
Then think not I am flothful in the race,
Or, that my Brother fprings before my Love.

ARSACES.

Far be fufpicion from me.

VARDANES.

So, 'tis done,
Thanks to diffembling, all is well again.

Q 2   KING

KING.

Now let us, forward, to the Temple go,
And let, with chearful wine, the goblets flow;
Let blink-ey'd Jollity his aid afford,
To crown our triumph, round the festive board:
But, let the wretch, whose soul can know a care,
Far from our joys, to some lone shade repair,
In secrecy, there let him e'er remain,
Brood o'er his gloom, and still increase his pain.

END of the FIRST ACT.

ACT

***

ACT II.   SCENE I.

A   P R I S O N.

LYSIAS, a'one.

THE Sun fet frowning, and refrefhing Eve
   Loft all its fweets, obfcur'd in double gloom.
This night fhall fleep be ftranger to thefe eyes,
Peace dwells not here, and flumber flies the fhock;
My fpirits, like the elements, are waring,
And mock the tempeft with a kindred rage———
I, who can joy in nothing, but revenge,
Know not thofe boafted ties of Love and Friendfhip;
Vardanes I regard, but as he gives me
Some hopes of vengeance on the Prince *Arfaces.*———
But, ha! he comes, wak'd by the angry ftorm,
'Tis to my wifh, thus would I form defigns,
Horror fhould breed beneath the veil of horror,
And darknefs aid confpiracies———He's here———

SCENE

SCENE II.

VARDANES and LYSIAS.

LYSIAS.

Welcome, my noble Prince.

VARDANES.

        Thanks, gentle friend ;
Heav'ns! what a night is this!

LYSIAS.

        'Tis fill'd with terror ;
Some dread event beneath this horror lurks,
Ordain'd by fate's irrevocable doom ;
Perhaps *Arſaces'* fall—and angry heav'n
Speaks it, in thunder, to the trembling world.

VARDANES.

Terror indeed! it ſeems as ſick'ning Nature
Had giv'n her order up to gen'ral ruin ;
The Heav'ns appear as one continu'd flame,
Earth with her terror ſhakes, dim night retires,
And the red lightning gives a dreadful day,
While in the thunder's voice each ſound is loſt ;
Fear ſinks the panting heart in ev'ry boſom,
E'en the pale dead, affrighted at the horror,

As

As tho' unfafe, ftart from their marble goals,
And howling thro' the ftreets are feeking fhelter.

LYSIAS.

I faw a flafh ftream thro' the angry clouds,
And bend its courfe to where a ftately pine
Behind the garden ftood, quickly it feiz'd,
And wrapt it in a fiery fold, the trunk
Was fhiver'd into atoms, and the branches
Off were lopt, and wildly fcatter'd round.

VARDANES.

Why rage the elements, they are not curs'd
Like me? *Evanthe* frowns not angry on them,
The wind may play upon her beauteous bofom
Nor fear her chiding, light can blefs her fenfe,
And in the floating mirror fhe beholds
Thofe beauties which can fetter all mankind.
Earth gives her joy, fhe plucks the fragrant rofe,
Pleas'd takes its fweets, and gazes on its bloom.

LYSIAS

My Lord, forget her, tear her from your breaft.
Who, like the *Phœnix*, gazes on the fun,
And ftrives to foar up to the glorious blaze,
Should never leave Ambition's brighteft object,
To turn, and view the beauties of a flow'r.

VARDANES.

VARDANES.

O, *Lysias*, chide no more, for, I have done.
Yes, I'll forget this proud disdainful beauty;
Hence, with, vain love——Ambition, now, alone,
Shall guide my actions, since mankind delights
To give me pain, I'll study mischief too,
And shake the earth, e'en like this raging tempest.

LYSIAS.

A night like this, so dreadful to behold,
Since my remembrance's birth, I never saw.

VARDANES.

E'en such a night, dreadful as this, they say,
My teeming Mother gave me to the world.
Whence by those sages who, in knowledge rich,
Can pry into futurity, and tell
What distant ages will produce of wonder,
My days were deem'd to be a hurricane;
My early life prov'd their prediction false;
Beneath a sky serene my voyage began,
But, to this long uninterrupted calm,
Storms shall succeed.

LYSIAS.

　　　　Then haste, to raise the tempest;
My soul disdains this one eternal round,
Where each succeeding day is like the former.

Trust

Truſt me, my noble Prince, here is a heart
Steady and firm to all your purpoſes,
And here's a hand that knows to execute
Whate'er deſigns thy daring breaſt can form,
Nor ever ſhake with fear.

VARDANES.

And I will uſe it,
Come to my boſom, let me place thee here,
How happy am I claſping ſo much virtue!
Now, by the light, it is my firm belief,
One mighty ſoul in common ſwells our boſoms,
Such ſameneſs can't be match'd in diff'rent beings.

LYSIAS.

Your confidence, my Lord, much honours me,
And when I act unworthy of your love
May I be hooted from Society,
As tho' diſgraceful to the human kind,
And driv'n to herd among the ſavage race.

VARDANES.

Believe me, *Lyſias*, I do not know
A ſingle thought which tends toward ſuſpicion,
For well I know thy worth, when I affront it,
By the leaſt doubt, may I be ever curs'd
With faithleſs friends, and by his dagger fall
Whom my deluded wiſhes moſt would favour.

R   LYSIAS.

Lysias.

Then let's no longer trifle time away,
I'm all impatience tell I see thy brows
Bright in the glories of a diadem;
My foul is fill'd with anguish when I think
That by weak Princes worn, 'tis thus difgrac'd.
Hafte, mount the throne, and, like the morning Sun,
Chace with your piercing beams thofe mifts away,
Which dim the glory of the *Parthian* ftate:
Each honeft heart defires it, numbers there are
Ready to join you, and fupport your caufe,
Againft th' oppofing faction.

Vardanes.

Sure fome God,
Bid you thus call me to my dawning honours,
And joyful I obey the pleafing fummons.
Now by the pow'rs of heav'n, of earth and hell,
Moft folemnly I fwear, I will not know
That quietude which I was wont to know,
'Til I have climb'd the height of all my wifhes,
Or fell, from glory, to the filent grave.

Lysias.

Nobly refolv'd, and fpoken like *Vardanes*,
There fhone my Prince in his fuperior luftre.

VARDANES.

But, then, *Arfaces*, he's a fatal bar——
O! could I brufh this bufy infect from me,
Which envious ftrives to rob me of my bloom,
Then might I, like fome fragrant op'ning flow'r,
Spread all my beauties in the face of day.
Ye Gods! why did ye give me fuch a foul,
(A foul, which ev'ry way is form'd for Empire)
And damn me with a younger Brother's right?
The diadem would fet as well on mine,
As on the brows of any lordly He;
Nor is this hand weak to enforce command,
And fhall I fteal into my grave, and give
My name up to oblivion, to be thrown
Among the common rubbifh of the times?
No: Perifh firft, this happy hated Brother.

LYSIAS.

I always wear a dagger, for your fervice,
I need not fpeak the reft——
When humbly I intreated of your Brother
T'attend him as Lieutenant in this war,
Frowning contempt, he haughtily reply'd,
He entertain'd not Traitors in his fervice.
True, I betray'd *Orodes*, but with caufe,
He ftruck me, like a forry abject flave,
And ftill withheld from giving what he'd promis'd.
Fear not *Arfaces*, believe me, he fhall

R 2

Soon

Soon his Quietus have—But, fee, he comes,——
What can this mean? Why at this lonely hour,
And unattended?—Ha! 'tis opportune—
I 'll in, and ftab him now. I heed not what
The danger is, fo I but have revenge,
Then heap perdition on me.

VARDANES.

Hold, awhile—
'Twould be better could we undermine him,
And make him fall by *Artabanus*' doom.

LYSIAS.

Well, be it fo—

VARDANES.

But let us now retire,
We muft not be obferv'd together here.

SCENE III.

ARSACES, alone.

'Tis here that haplefs *Bethas* is confin'd;
He who, but yefterday, like angry Jove,
When punifhing the crimes of guilty men,
Spread death and defolation all around,
While PARTHIA trembl'd at his name; is now

Unfriended

Unfriended and forlorn, and counts the hours,
Wrapt in the gloomy horrors of a goal.——
How dark, and hidden, are the turns of fate!
His rigid fortune moves me to compassion.
O! 'tis a heav'nly virtue when the heart
Can feel the sorrows of another's bosom,
It dignifies the man: The stupid wretch
Who knows not this sensation, is an image,
And wants the feeling to make up a life——
I 'll in, and give my aid to sooth his sorrows.

SCENE IV.

VARDANES and LYSIAS.

LYSIAS.

Let us observe with care, something we, yet,
May gather, to give to us the vantage;
No matter what 's the intent.

VARDANES.

How easy 'tis
To cheat this busy, tattling, censuring world!
For fame still names our actions, good or bad,
As introduc'd by chance, which ofttimes throws
Wrong lights on objects; vice she dresses up

In the bright form, and goodlineſs, of virtue,
While virtue languiſhes, and pines neglected,
Rob'd of her luſtre—But, let's forward *Lyſias*—
Thou know'ſt each turn in this thy dreary rule,
Then lead me to ſome ſecret ſtand, from whence,
Unnotic'd, all their actions we may view.

LYSIAS.

Here, take your ſtand behind—See, *Bethas* comes.

[*They retire.*]

SCENE V.

BETHAS, alone.

To think on Death, in gloomy ſolitude,
In dungeons and in chains, when expectation
Join'd with ſerious thought deſcribe him to us,
His height'n'd terrors ſtrike upon the ſoul
With awful dread; imagination rais'd
To frenzy, plunges in a ſea of horror,
And taſtes the pains, the agonies of dying—
Ha! who is this, perhaps he bears my fate?
It muſt be ſo, but, why this **privacy**?

SCENE

SCENE VI.

Arsaces and Bethas.

ARSACES.

Health to the noble *Bethas*, health and joy!

BETHAS.

A steady harden'd villain, one experienc'd
In his employment ; ha! where's thy dagger?
It cannot give me fear; I'm ready, see,
My op'ning bosom tempts the friendly steel.
Fain would I cast this tiresome being off,
Like an old garment worn to wretchedness.
Here, strike for I'm prepar'd.

ARSACES.

Oh! view me better,
Say, do I wear the gloomy ruffian's frown?

BETHAS.

Ha! 'tis the gallant Prince, the brave *Arsaces*,
And *Bethas'* Conqueror.

ARSACES.

And *Bethas'* friend,
A name I'm proud to wear.

BETHAS.

BETHAS.

Away—away—

Mock with your jester to divert the court,
Fit Scene for sportive joys and frolic mirth;
Thinkst thou I lack that manly constancy
Which braves misfortune, and remains unshaken?
Are these, are these the emblems of thy friendship,
These rankling chains, say, does it gall like these?
No, let me taste the bitterness of sorrow,
For I am reconcil'd to wretchedness.
The Gods have empty'd all their mighty store,
Of hoarded Ills, upon my whiten'd age;
Now death—but, oh! I court coy death in vain,
Like a cold maid, he scorns my fond complaining.
'Tis thou, insulting Prince, 'tis thou hast dragg'd
My soul, just rising, down again to earth,
And clogg'd her wings with dull mortality,
A hateful bondage! Why—

ARSACES.

A moment hear me—

BETHAS.

Why dost thou, like an angry vengeful ghost,
Glide hither to disturb this peaceful gloom?
What, dost thou envy me my miseries,
My chains and flinty pavement, where I oft
In sleep behold the image of the death I wish,

Forget

Forget my forrows and heart-breaking anguish?
Thefe horrors I would undifturb'd enjoy,
Attended only by my filent thoughts;
Is it to fee the wretch that you have made,
To view the ruins of unhappy *Bethas*,
And triumph in my grief? Is it for this
You penetrate my dark joylefs prifon?

ARSACES.

Oh! do not injure me by fuch fufpicions.
Unknown to me are cruel fcoffs and jefts;
My breaft can feel compaffion's tendernefs,
The warrior's warmth, the foothing joys of friendfhip.
When adverfe bold battalions fhook the earth,
And horror triumph'd on the hoftile field,
I fought you with a glorious enmity,
And arm'd my brow with the ftern frown of war.
But now the angry trumpet wakes no more
The youthful champion to the luft for blood.
Retiring rage gives place to fofter paffions,
And gen'rous warriors know no longer hate,
The name of foe is loft, and thus I afk
Your friendfhip.

BETHAS.

Ah! why doft thou mock me thus?

S ARSACES.

ARSACES.

Let the bafe coward, he who ever fhrinks,
And trembles, at the flight name of danger,
Taunt, and revile, with bitter gibes, the wretched;
The brave are ever to diftrefs a friend.
Tho' my dear country, (fpoil'd by wafteful war,
Her harvefts blazing, defolate her towns,
And baleful ruin fhew'd her hagard face)
Call'd out on me to fave her from her foes,
And I obey'd, yet to your gallant prowefs,
And unmatch'd deeds, I admiration gave.
But now my country knows the fweets of fafety,
Freed from her fears; fure now I may indulge
My juft efteem for your fuperior virtue.

BETHAS.

Yes, I muft think you what you would be thought,
For honeft minds are eafy of belief,
And always judge of others by themfelves,
But often are deceiv'd; yet *Parthia* breeds not
Virtue much like thine, the barb'rous clime teems
With nought elfe but villains vers'd in ill.

ARSACES

Diffimulation never mark'd my looks,
Nor flatt'ring deceit e'er taught my tongue,
The tale of falfhood, to difguife my thoughts:
To Virtue, and, her fair companion, Truth,

I've

I've ever bow'd, their holy precepts kept,
And scann'd by them the actions of my life.
Suspicion surely ne'er disturbs the brave,
They never know the fears of doubting thoughts;
But free, as are the altars of the Gods,
From ev'ry hand receive the sacrafice.

SCENE VII.

ARSACES, BETHAS EVANTHE and CLEONE.

EVANTHE.

Heav'ns! what a gloom hangs round this dreadful place,
Fit habitation for the guilty mind!
Oh! if such terrors wait the innocent,
Which tread these vaults, what must the impious feel,
Who've all their crimes to stare them in the face?

BETHAS.

Immortal Gods! is this reality?
Or meer illusion? am I bleft at laft,
Or is it to torment me that you've rais'd
This semblance of *Evanthe* to my eyes?
It is! it is! 'tis she!———

ARSACES.

Ha!—what means this?—

S 2

She

She faints! fhe faints! life has forfook its feat,
Pale Death ufurps its place—*Evanthe*, Oh!
Awake to life!—Love and *Arfaces* call!—

BETHAS.

Off— give her to my arms, my warm embrace
Shall melt Death's icy chains.

CLEONE.

　　　　　She lives! fhe lives!—
See, on her cheeks the rofy glow returns.

ARSACES.

O joy! O joy! her op'ning eyes, again,
Break, like the morning fun, a better day.

BETHAS.

Evanthe!—

EVANTHE.

Oh! my Father!—

ARSACES.

Ha!—her Father!

BETHAS.

Heav'n thou art kind at laft, and this indeed
Is recompenfe for all the ills I've paft;

　　　　　　　　　　　　　　　　For

For all the forrows which my heart has known,
Each wakeful night, and ev'ry day of anguifh.
This, this has fweet'n'd all my bitter cup,
And gave me once again to tafte of joy,
Joy which has long been ftranger to this bofom.
Hence—hence difgrace—off, ignominy off—
But one embrace—I afk but one embrace,
And 'tis deny'd.

EVANTHE.

O, yes, around thy neck
I'll fold my longing arms, thy fofter fetters,
Thus prefs thee to my happy breaft, and kifs
Away thofe tears that ftain thy aged cheeks.

BETHAS.

Oh! 'tis too much! it is too much! ye Gods!
Life's at her utmoft ftretch, and burfting near
With heart-fwoln ecftafy; now let me die.

ARSACES.

What marble heart
Could fee this fcene unmov'd, nor give a tear?
My eyes grow dim, and fympathetic paffion
Falls like a gufhing torrent on my bofom.

EVANTHE.

O! happy me, this place, which lately feem'd
So fill'd with horror, now is pleafure's circle.

Here will I fix my feat; my pleafing tafk
Shall be to cherifh thy remaining life.
All night I 'll keep a vigil o'er thy flumbers,
And on my breaft repofe thee, mark thy dreams,
And when thou wak'ft invent fome pleafing tale,
Or with my fongs the tedious hours beguile.

BETHAS.

Still let me gaze, ftill let me gaze upon thee,
Let me ftrain ev'ry nerve with ravifhment,
And all my life be center'd in my vifion.
To fee thee thus, to hear thy angel voice,
It is, indeed, a luxury of pleafure!——
Speak, fpeak again, for oh! 'tis heav'n to hear thee!
Celeftial fweetnefs dwells on ev'ry accent;——
Lull me to reft, and footh my raging joy.
Joy which diftracts me with unruly tranfports.
Now, by thy dear departed Mother's fhade,
Thou brighteft pattern of all excellence,
Thou who in prattling infancy haft bleft me,
I wou'd not give this one tranfporting moment,
This fullnefs of delight, for all——but, ah!
,Tis vile, Ambition, Glory, all is vile,
To the foft fweets of love and tendernefs.

EVANTHE.

Now let me fpeak, my throbbing heart is full,

I 'll

I'll tell thee all—alas! I have forgot—
'T'as flipt me in the tumult of my joy.
And yet I thought that I had much to fay.

BETHAS.

Oh! I have curs'd my birth, indeed, I have
Blasphem'd the Gods, with unbecoming paffion,
Arraign'd their Juftice, and defy'd their pow'r,
In bitternefs, becaufe they had deny'd
Thee to fupport the weaknefs of my age.
But now no more I'll rail and rave at fate,
All its decrees are juft, complaints are impious.
Whate'er fhort-fighted mortals feel, fprings from
Their blindnefs in the ways of Providence;
Sufficient wifdom 'tis for man to know
That the great Ruler is e'er wife and good.

ARSACES.

Ye figur'd ftones!
Ye fenfelefs, lifelefs images of men,
Who never gave a tear to others woe,
Whofe bofoms never glow'd for others good,
O weary heav'n with your repeated pray'rs,
And ftrive to melt the angry pow'rs to pity,
That ye may truly live.

EVANTHE.

Oh! how my heart
Beats in my breaft, and fhakes my trembling frame!

I fink beneath this fudden flood of joy,
Too mighty for my fpirits.

ARSACES.

My *Evanthe*,
Thus in my arms I catch thy falling beauties,
Chear thee; and kifs thee back to life again:
Thus to my bofom I could ever hold thee,
And find new pleafure.

EVANTHE.

O! my lov'd, *Arfaces*,
Forgive me that I faw thee not before,
Indeed my foul was bufily employ'd,
Nor left a fingle thought at liberty.
But thou, I know, art gentlenefs and love.
Now I am doubly paid for all my forrows,
For all my fears for thee.

ARSACES.

Then, fear no more:
Give to guilty wretches painful terrors:
Whofe keen remembrance raifes horrid forms,
Shapes that in fpite of nature fhock their fouls
With dreadful anguifh: but thy gentle bofom,
Where innocence beams light and gayety,
Can never know a fear, now fhining joy
Shall gild the pleafing fcene.

EVANTHE.

EVANTHE.

Alas ! this joy
I fear is like a fudden flame fhot from
Th' expiring taper, darknefs will enfue,
And double night I dread enclofe us round.
Anxiety does yet difturb my breaft,
And frightful apprehenfion fhakes my foul.

BETHAS.

How fhall I thank you, ye bright glorious beings!
Shall I in humble adoration bow,
Or fill the earth with your refounding praife ?
No, this I leave to noify hypocrites,
A Mortal's tongue difgraces fuch a theme;
But heav'n delights where filent gratitude
Mounts each afpiring thought to its bright throne,
Nor leaves to language aught; words may indeed
From man to man their fev'ral wants exprefs,
Heav'n afks the purer incenfe of the heart.

ARSACES.

I'll to the King, 'ere he retires to reft,
Nor will I leave him 'til I 've gain'd your freedom ;
His love will furely not deny me this.

T   SCENE

SCENE VIII.

VARDANES and LYSIAS (come forward.)

LYSIAS.

'Twas a moving Scene, e'en my rough nature
Was nighly melted.

VARDANES.

Hence coward pity——
What is joy to them, to me is torture.
Now am I rack'd with pains that far exceed
Those agonies, which fabling Priests relate,
The damn'd endure: The shock of hopeless Love,
Unblest with any views to sooth ambition,
Rob me of all my reas'ning faculties.
Arsaces gains *Evanthe*, fills the throne,
While I am doom'd to foul obscurity,
To pine and grieve neglected.

LYSIAS.

My noble Prince,
Would it not be a master-piece, indeed,
To make this very bliss their greatest ill,
And damn them in the very folds of joy?

VARDANES.

This I will try, and stretch my utmost art,

Unknown

Unknown is yet the means—We'll think on that——
Succefs may follow if you'll lend your aid.

LYSIAS.

The ftorm ftill rages——I muft to the King,
And know what further orders 'ere he fleeps:
Soon I'll return, and fpeak my mind more fully.

VARDANES.

Hafte, *Lyfias*, hafte, to aid me with thy council ;
For without thee, all my defigns will prove
Like night and chaos, darknefs and confufion ;
But to thy word fhall light and order fpring.——
Let coward Schoolmen talk of Virtue's rules,
And preach the vain Philofophy of fools ;
Court eager their obfcurity, afraid
To tafte a joy, and in fome gloomy fhade
Dream o'er their lives, while in a mournful ftrain
They fing of happinefs, they never gain.
But form'd for nobler purpofes I come,
To gain a crown, or elfe a glorious tomb.

END of the SECOND ACT.

T 2   ACT

ACT III.   *SCENE* I.

The P A L A C E.

QUEEN and EDESSA.

QUEEN.

TALK not of fleep to me, the God of Reft
   Difdains to vifit where diforder reigns;
Not beds of down, nor mufic's fofteft ftrains,
Can charm him when 'tis anarchy within.
He flies with eager hafte the mind difturb'd,
And fheds his bleffings where the foul's in peace.

EDESSA.

Yet, hear me, Madam!

QUEEN.

Hence, away, *Edeffa*,
For thou know'ft not the pangs of jealoufy.
Say, has he not forfook my bed, and left me
Like a lone widow mourning to the night?
This, with the injury his fon has done me,

If

If I forgive, may heav'n in anger fhow'r
Its torments on me——Ha! is n't that the King?

EDESSA.

It is your Royal Lord, great *Artabanus.*

QUEEN.

Leave me, for I would meet him here alone,
Something is lab'ring in my breaft——

SCENE II.

KING and QUEEN.

KING.

This leads
To fair *Evanthe's* chamber——Ha! the Queen.

QUEEN.

Why doft thou ftart? fo ftarts the guilty wretch,
When, by fome watchful eye, prevented from
His dark defigns.

KING.

Prevented! how, what mean'ft thou?

QUEEN.

Art thou then fo dull? cannot thy heart,
Thy changeling heart, explain my meaning to thee,
Or muft upbraiding 'wake thy apprehenfion?
Ah! faithlefs, tell me, have I loft thofe charms
Which thou fo oft haft fworn could warm old age,
And tempt the frozen hermit from his cell,
To vifit once again our gayer world?
This, thou haft fworn, perfidious as thou art,
A thoufand times; as often haft thou fworn
Eternal conftancy, and endlefs love,
Yet ev'ry time was perjur'd.

KING.

Sure, 'tis frenzy.

QUEEN.

Indeed, 'tis frenzy, 'tis the height of madnefs,
For I have wander'd long in fweet delufion.
At length the pleafing Phantom chang'd its form,
And left me in a wildernefs of woe.

KING.

Prithee, no more, difmifs thofe jealous heats;
Love muft decay, and foon difguft arife,
Where endlefs jarrings and upbraidings damp
The gentle flame, which warms the lover's breaft.

QUEEN.

QUEEN.

Oh! grant me patience heav'n! and doft thou think
By thefe reproaches to difguife thy guilt?
No, tis in vain, thy art's too thin to hide it.

KING.

Curfe on the marriage chain!—the clog, a wife,
Who ftill will force and pall us with the joy,
Tho' pow'r is wanting, and the will is cloy'd,
Still urge the debt when Nothing's left to pay.

QUEEN.

Ha! doft thou own thy crime, nor feel the glow
Of confcious fhame?

KING.

Why fhould I blufh, If heav'n
Has made me as I am, and gave me paffions?
Bleft only in variety, then blame
The Gods, who form'd my nature thus, not me.

QUEEN.

Oh! Traitor! Villain!

KING.

Hence—away—
No more I'll wage a woman's war with words.   [*Exit.*]

QUEEN.

Down, down ye rifing paffions, give me eafe,

Or

Or break my heart, for I muſt yet be calm.—
But, yet, revenge, our Sex's joy, is mine;
By all the Gods! he lives not till the morn.
Who ſlights my love, ſhall ſink beneath my hate.

SCENE III.

QUEEN and VARDANES.

VARDANES.

What, raging to the tempeſt?

QUEEN.

Away!—away!——
Yes, I will rage—a tempeſt's here within,
Above the trifling of the noiſy elements.
Blow ye loud winds, burſt with your violence,
For ye but barely imitate the ſtorm
That wildly rages in my tortur'd breaſt—
The King—the King—

VARDANES.

Ha! what?—the King?

QUEEN.

Evanthe!—

VARDANES.

VARDANES.

You talk like riddles, ftill obfcure and fhort,
Give me fome cue to guide me thro' this maze.

QUEEN.

Ye pitying pow'rs!—oh! for a poifon, fome
Curs'd deadly draught, that I might blaft her beauties,
And rob her eyes of all their fatal luftre.

VARDANES.

What, blaft her charms?—dare not to think of it—
Shocking impiety;—the num'rous fyftems
Which gay creation fpreads, bright blazing funs,
With all th' attendant planets circling round,
Are not worth half the radiance of her eyes.
She's heav'n's peculiar care, good fpir'ts hover
Round, a fhining band, to guard her beauties.

QUEEN.

Be they watchful then; for fhould remifsnefs
Taint the guard, I'll fnatch the opportunity,
And hurl her to deftruction.

VARDANES.

Dread *Thermufa*,
Say, what has rous'd this tumult in thy foul?
Why doft thou rage with unabating fury,
Wild as the winds, loud as the troubl'd fea?

U

QUEEN.

Yes, I will tell thee——*Evanthe*——curfe her——
With charms——Would that my curfes had the pow'r
To kill, deftroy, and blaft where e'er I hate,
Then would I curfe, ftill curfe, till death fhould feize
The dying accents on my falt'ring tongue,
So fhould this world, and the falfe changeling man
Be buried in one univerfal ruin.

VARDANES.

Still err'ft thou from the purpofe.

QUEEN.

Ha! 'tis fo——
Yes I will tell thee——for I know fond fool,
Deluded wretch, thou doteft on *Evanthe*——
Be that thy greateft curfe, be curs'd like me,
With jealoufy and rage, for know, the King,
Thy father, is thy rival.

SCENE IV.

VARDANES, alone.

Ha! my rival!
How knew fhe that?—yet ftay—fhe's gone—my rival,
What then? he is *Arfaces'* rival too.
Ha!—this may aid and ripen my defigns——

Could

Could I but fire the King with jealoufy,
And then accufe my Brother of Intrigues
Againſt the ſtate—ha!—join'd with *Bethas*, and
Confed'rate with th' Arabians—'tis moſt likely
That jealoufy would urge him to belief.
I'll ſink my claim until ſome fitter time,
'Til opportunity ſmiles on my purpoſe.
Lyſias' already has receiv'd the mandate
For *Bethas'* freedom: Let them ſtill proceed,
This harmony ſhall change to diſcord ſoon.
Fortune methinks of late grows wond'rous kind,
She ſcarcely leaves me to employ myſelf.

SCENE V.

KING, ARSACES, VARDANES.

KING.

But where's *Evanthe?* Where's the lovely Maid?

ARSACES.

On the cold pavement, by her aged Sire,
The dear companion of his ſolitude,
She ſits, nor can perſuaſion make her riſe;
But in the wild extravagance of joy
She weeps, then ſmiles, like April's ſun, thro' ſhow'rs.

While

While with ſtrain'd eyes he gazes on her face,
And cries, in ecſtacy, "Ye gracious pow'rs!
"It is too much, it is too much to bear!"
Then claſps her to his breaſt, while down his cheeks
Large drops each other trace, and mix with hers.

K<small>ING</small>.

Thy tale is moving, for my eyes o'erflow—
How ſlow does *Lyſias* with *Evanthe* creep!
So moves old time when bringing us to bliſs.
Now war ſhall ceaſe, no more of war I'll have,
Death knows ſatiety, and pale deſtruction
Turns loathing from his food, thus forc'd on him.
The triffling duſt, the cauſe of all this ruin,
The trade of death ſhall urge no more.—

S C E N E VI.

K<small>ING</small>, A<small>RSACES</small>, V<small>ARDANES</small>, E<small>VANTHE</small>, L<small>YSIAS</small>.

K<small>ING</small>.

Evanthe !—

See pleaſure's goddeſs deigns to dignify
The happy ſcene, and make our bliſs complete.
So *Venus*, from her heav'nly ſeat, deſcends
To bleſs the gay *Cythera* with her preſence;

A

A thoufand fmiling graces wait the goddefs,
A thoufand little loves are flutt'ring round,
And joy is mingl'd with the beauteous train.

EVANTHE.

O! Royal Sir, thus lowly to the ground
I bend, in humble gratitude, accept
My thanks, for this thy goodnefs, words are vile
T' exprefs the image of my lively thought,
And fpeak the grateful fulnefs of my heart.
All I can fay, is that I now am happy,
And that thy giving hand has made me bleft.

KING.

O! rife, *Evanthe* rife, this lowly pofture
Suits not with charms like thine, they fhould command,
And ev'ry heart exult in thy behefts;—
But, where's thy aged Sire?

EVANTHE.

This fudden turn
Of fortune has fo wrought upon his frame,
His limbs could not fupport him to thy prefence.

ARSACES.

This, this is truly great, this is the Hero,
Like heav'n, to fcatter bleffings 'mong mankind,
And e'er delight in making others happy.

Cold is the praise which waits the victor's triumph,
(Who thro' a sea of blood has rush'd to glory),
To the o'erflowings of a grateful heart,
By obligations conquer'd : Yet, extend
Thy bounty unto me. [Kneels]

KING.

Ha! rise *Arsaces*.

ARSACES.

Not till you grant my boon.

KING.

Speak, and 'tis thine—
Wide thro' our kingdom let thy eager wishes
Search for some jewel worthy of thy seeing;
Something that's fit to show the donor's bounty,
And by the glorious sun, our worship'd God,
Thou shalt not have denial; e'en my crown
Shall gild thy brows with shining beams of Empire.
With pleasure I'll resign to thee my honours,
I long for calm retirement's softer joys.

ARSACES.

Long may you wear it, grant it bounteous heav'n,
And happiness attend it ; 'tis my pray'r
That daily rises with the early sweets
Of nature's incense, and the lark's loud strain.

'Tis

'Tis not the unruly tranſport of ambition
That urges my deſires to aſk your crown;
Let the vain wretch, who prides in gay dominion,
Who thinks not of the great ones weighty cares,
Enjoy his lofty wiſh, wide ſpreading rule.
The treaſure which I aſk, put in the ſcale,
Would over-balance all that Kings can boaſt,
Empire and diadems.

KING.

Away, that thought—
Name it, haſte—ſpeak.

ARSACES.

For all the dang'rous toil,
Thirſt, hunger, marches long that I've endur'd,
For all the blood I've in thy ſervice ſpent,
Reward me with *Evanthe.*

KING.

Ha! what ſaid'ſt thou?—

VARDANES.

The King is mov'd, and angry bites his lip.—
Thro' my benighted ſoul all-chearing hope   [Aſide.]
Beams, like an orient ſun, reviving joy.

ARSACES.

ARSACES.

The ſtern *Vonones* ne'er could boaſt a merit
But loving her.

KING.

        Ah! curſe the hated name—
Yes, I remember when the fell ruffian
Directed all his fury at my life;
Then ſent, by pitying heav'n, t' aſſert the right
Of injur'd Majeſty, thou, *Arſaces*,
Taught him the duty he ne'er knew before,
And laid the Traitor dead.

ARSACES.

My Royal Sire!

LYSIAS.

My Liege, the Prince ſtill kneels.

KING.

        Ha!—rebel, off—   [Strikes him]
What, *Lyſias*, did I ſtrike thee? forgive my rage—
The name of curs'd *Vonones* fires my blood,
And gives me up to wrath.—

LYSIAS.

        I am your ſlave,
Sway'd by your pleaſure—when I forget it,

                             May

May this keen dagger, which I mean to hide,
Deep in his bofom, pierce my vitals thro'.   [Afide]

KING.

Did'ft thou not name *Evanthe?*

ARSACES.

I did, my Lord!
And, fay, whom fhould I name but her, in whom
My foul has center'd all her happinefs?
Nor can'ft thou blame me, view her wond'rous charms,
She's all perfection; bounteous heav'n has form'd her
To be the joy, and wonder of mankind;
But language is too vile to fpeak her beauties,
Here ev'ry pow'r of glowing fancy's loft:
Rofe blufh fecure, ye lilies ftill enjoy
Your filver whitenefs, I'll not rob your charms
To deck the bright comparifon; for here
It fure muft fail.

KING.

He's wanton in her praife—   [Afide]
I tell thee, Prince, hadft thou as many tongues,
As days have wafted fince creation's birth,
They were too few to tell the mighty theme.

EVANTHE.

I'm loft! I'm loft!   [Afide]

                    X   ARSACES.

ARSACES.

Then I'll be dumb for ever.

KING.

O rafh and fatal oath! is there no way,
No winding path to fhun this precipice,
But muft I fall and dafh my hopes to atoms?
In vain I ftrive, thought but perplexes me,
Yet fhews no hold to bear me up—now, hold
My heart a while—fhe's thine—'tis done.

ARSACES.

In deep
Proftration, I thank my Royal Father.

KING.

A fudden pain fhoots thro' my trembling breaft—
Lend me thy arm *Vardanes*—cruel pow'rs!

SCENE VII.

ARSACES, and EVANTHE.

EVANTHE, (after a paufe)
E'er fince the dawn of my unhappy life
Joy never fhone ferenely on my foul;
Still fomething interven'd to cloud my day.

Tell

Tell me, ye pow'rs, unfold the hidden crime
For which I'm doom'd to this eternal woe,
Thus still to number o'er my hours with tears?
The Gods are juft I know, nor are decrees
In hurry fhuffl'd out, but where the bolt
Takes its direction juftice points the mark.
Yet ftill in vain I fearch within my breaft,
I find no fins are there to fhudder at—
Nought but the common frailties of our natures.
Arfaces,—Oh!—

ARSACES.

Ha! why that look of anguifh?
Why didft thou name me with that found of forrow?
Ah! fay, why ftream thofe gufhing tears fo faft
From their bright fountain? fparkling joy fhould now
Be lighten'd in thine eye, and pleafure glow
Upon thy rofy cheek;—ye forrows hence—
'Tis love fhall triumph now.

EVANTHE.

Oh!   [Sighs]

ARSACES.

What means that figh?
Tell me why heaves thy breaft with fuch emotion?
Some dreadful thought is lab'ring for a vent,
Hafte, give it loofe, 'ere ftrengthen'd by confinement

X 2

It

It wrecks thy frame, and tears its fnowy prifon.
Is forrow then fo pleafing that you hoard it
With as much love, as mifers do their gold?
Give me my fhare of forrows.

EVANTHE.

Ah! too foon
You 'll know what I would hide.

ARSACES.

Be it from thee——
The dreadful tale, when told by thee, fhall pleafe;
Hafte, to produce it with its native terrors,
My fteady foul fhall ftill remain unfhaken;
For who when blefs'd with beauties like to thine
Would e'er permit a forrow to intrude?
Far hence in darkfome fhades does forrow dwell,
Where haplefs wretches thro' the awful gloom,
Echo their woes, and fighing to the winds,
Augment with tears the gently murm'ring ftream;
But ne'er difturbs fuch happinefs as mine.

EVANTHE.

Oh! 'tis not all thy boafted happinefs,
Can fave thee from difquietude and care;
Then build not too fecurely on thefe joys,
For envious forrow foon will undermine,
And let the goodly ftructure fall to ruin.

ARSACES,

ARSACES.

I charge thee, by our mutual vows, *Evanthe*,
Tell me, nor longer keep me in fufpenfe:
Give me to know the utmoft rage of fate.

EVANTHE.

Then know——impoffible !—

ARSACES.

Ha ! doft thou fear
To fhock me ?———

EVANTHE.

Know, thy Father——loves *Evanthe*.—

ARSACES.

Loves thee?

EVANTHE.

Yea, e'en to diftraction loves me.
Oft at my feet he's told the moving tale,
And woo'd me with the ardency of youth.
I pitied him indeed, but that was all,
Thou would'ft have pitied too.

ARSACES.

I fear 'tis true ;
A thoufand crouding circumftances fpeak it.

Ye

Ye cruel Gods! I've wreck'd a Father's peace,
Oh! bitter thought!

EVANTHE.

   Didſt thou obſerve, *Arſaces*,
How reluctant he gave me to thy arms?

ARSACES.

Yes, I obſerv'd that when he gave thee up,
It ſeem'd as tho' he gave his precious life.
And who'd forego the heav'n of thy love?
To reſt on thy ſoft ſwelling breaſt, and, in
Sweet ſlumbers ſooth each ſharp intruding care?
Oh! it were bliſs, ſuch as immortals taſte,
To preſs thy ruby lips diſtilling ſweets,
Or circl'd in thy ſnowy arms to ſnatch
A joy, that Gods—

EVANTHE.

   Come, then, my much-lov'd Prince,
Let's ſeek the ſhelter of ſome kind retreat.
Happy Arabia opens wide her arms,
There may we find ſome friendly ſolitude,
Far from the noiſe and hurry of the Court.
Ambitious views ſhall never blaſt our joys,
Or tyrant Fathers triumph o'er our wills:
There may we live like the firſt happy pair
Cloath'd in primeval innocence ſecure.

          Our

Our food untainted by luxurious arts,
Plain, simple, as our lives, shall not destroy
The health it should sustain; while the clear brook
Affords the cooling draught our thirsts to quench.
There, hand in hand, we'll trace the citron grove,
While with the songsters' round I join my voice,
To hush thy cares and calm thy ruffl'd soul:
Or, on some flow'ry bank reclin'd, my strains
Shall captivate the natives of the stream,
While on its crystal lap ourselves we view.

ARSACES.

I see before us a wide sea of sorrows,
Th' angry waves roll forward to o'erwhelm us,
Black clouds arise, and the wind whistles loud.
But yet, oh! could I save thee from the wreck,
Thou beauteous casket, where my joys are stor'd,
Let the storm rage with double violence,
Smiling I'd view its wide extended horrors.

EVANTHE.

'Tis not enough that we do know the ill,
Say, shall we calmly see the tempest rise,
And seek no shelter from th' inclement sky,
But bid it rage?—

ARSACES.

Ha! will he force thee from me?

What,

What, tear thee from my fond and bleeding heart?
And muft I lofe thee ever? dreadful word!
Never to gaze upon thy beauties more?
Never to taſte the fweetnefs of thy lips?
Never to know the joys of mutual love?
Never!—Oh! let me lofe the pow'r of thinking,
For thought is near allied to defperation.
Why, cruel Sire—why did you give me life,
And load it with a weight of wretchednefs?
Take back my being, or relieve my forrows—
Ha! art thou not *Evanthe?*—Art thou not
The lovely Maid, who blefs'd the fond *Arſaces?*—   [Raving.]

EVANTHE.

O, my lov'd Lord, recall your fcatter'd fpir'ts,
Alas! I fear your fenfes are unfettl'd.

ARSACES.

Yes, I would leave this dull and heavy fenfe.
Let me grow mad; perhaps, I then may gain
Some joy, by kind imagination form'd,
Beyond reality.—O! my *Evanthe!*
Why was I curs'd with empire? born to rule?—
Would I had been fome humble Peafant's fon,
And thou fome Shepherd's daughter on the plain;
My throne fome hillock, and my flock my fubjects,
My crook my fceptre, and my faithful dog
My only guard; nor curs'd with dreams of greatnefs.

At

At early dawn I'd hail the coming day,
And join the lark the rival of his lay;
At fultry noon to fome kind fhade repair,
Thus joyful pafs the hours, my only care,
To guard my flock, and pleafe the yielding Fair.

SCENE VIII.

KING.——VARDANES, behind the *Scene.*

KING.

I will not think, to think is torment—Ha!
See, how they twine! ye furies cut their hold.
Now their hot blood beats loud to love's alarms;
Sigh preffes figh, while from their fparkling eyes
Flafhes defire——Oh! ye bright heav'nly beings,
Who pitying bend to fuppliant Lovers pray'rs,
And aid them in extremity, affift me!

VARDANES.

Thus, for the Trojan, mourn'd the Queen of Carthage;
So, on the fhore fhe raving ftood, and faw
His navy leave her hofpitable fhore.
In vain fhe curs'd the wind which fill'd their fails,
And bore the emblem of its change away. [Comes forward.]

Y KING.

KING.

Vardanes—ha!—come here, I know thou lov'ſt me.

VARDANES.

I do my Lord; but, ſay, what buſy villain
Durſt e'er approach your ear, with coz'ning tales,
And urge you to a doubt?

KING.

          None, none believe me.
I'll ne'er oppreſs thy love with fearful doubt—
A little nigher—let me lean upon thee—
And thou be my ſupport—for now I mean
T' unboſom to thee free without reſtraint:
Search all the deep receſſes of my ſoul,
And open ev'ry darling thought before thee,
Which long I've ſecreted with jealous care.
Pray, mark me well.

VARDANES.

        I will, my Royal Sire.

KING.

On *Anna* thus reclin'd the love-ſick Dido;
Thus to her cheek laid hers with gentle preſſure,
And wet her ſiſter with a pearly ſhow'r,
Which fell from her ſad eyes, then told her tale,
While gentle *Anna* gave a pitying tear,

                            And

And own'd 'twas moving—thou canſt pity too,
I know thy nature tender and engaging.

VARDANES.

Tell me, my gracious Lord, what moves you thus?
Why is your breaſt diſtracted with theſe tumults?
Teach me ſome method how to ſooth your ſorrows,
And give your heart its former peace and joy;
Inſtruct, thy lov'd, *Vardanes.*——

KING.

Yes, I'll tell thee;
But liſten with attention while I ſpeak;
And yet I know 'twill ſhock thy gentle ſoul,
And horror o'er thee 'll ſpread his palſy hand.
O, my lov'd Son! thou fondneſs of my age!
Thou art the prop of my declining years,
In thee alone I find a Father's joy,
Of all my offſpring: But *Arſaces*——

VARDANES.

Ha!
My Brother!—

KING.

Ay—why doſt ſtart?—thy Brother
Purſues me with his hate: and, while warm life
Rolls the red current thro' my veins, delights

Y 2

To fee me tortur'd; with an eafy fmile
He meets my fuff'rings, and derides my pain.

VARDANES.

Oh!

KING.

What means that hollow groan?—*Vardanes*, fpeak,
Death's image fits upon thy pallid cheek,
While thy low voice founds as when murmurs run
Thro' lengthen'd vaults—

VARDANES.

O! my foreboding thoughts,   [Afide]
'Twas this difturb'd my reft; when fleep at night
Lock'd me in flumbers; in my dreams I faw
My Brother's crime—yet, death!—it cannot be—

KING.

Ha!—what was that?—

VARDANES.

O! my dread Lord, fome Villain
Bred up in lies, and train'd to treach'ry,
Has injur'd you by vile reports, to ftain
My Princely Brother's honour.

KING.
Thou know'ft more,

Thy

Thy looks confefs what thou in vain wouldft hide——
And haft thou then confpir'd againft me too,
And fworn concealment to your practices?——
Thy guilt——

VARDANES.

Ha! guilt!—what guilt?——

KING.

Nay, ftart not fo——
I'll know your purpofes, fpite of thy art.

VARDANES.

O! ye great Gods! and is it come to this?——
My Royal Father call your reafon home,
Drive thefe loud paffions hence, that thus deform you,
My Brother—Ah! what fhall I fay?—My Brother
Sure loves you as he ought.

KING.

Ha! as he ought?—
Hell blifter thy evafive tongue—I'll know it—
I will; I'll fearch thy breaft, thus will I open
A paffage to your fecrets—yet refolv'd——
Yet fteady in your horrid villany——
'Tis fit that I from whom fuch monfters fprung
No more fhould burthen earth—Ye Parricides!——
Here plant your daggers in this hated bofom ——

Here

Here rive my heart, and end at once my`forrows,
I gave ye being, that's the mighty crime.

VARDANES.

I can no more—here let me bow in anguifh——
Think not that I e'er join'd in his defigns,
Becaufe I have conceal'd my knowledge of them;
I meant, by pow'rful reafon's friendly aid,
To turn him from deftruction's dreadful path,
And bring him to a fenfe of what he ow'd
To you as King and Father.

KING.

Say on—I'll hear.

VARDANES.

He views thy facred life with envious hate,
As 'tis a bar to his ambitious hopes.
On the bright throne of Empire his plum'd wifhes
Seat him, while on his proud afpiring brows
He feels the pleafing weight of Royalty.
But when he wakes from thefe his airy dreams,
(Delufions form'd by the deceiver hope,
To raife him to the glorious height of greatnefs)
Then hurl him from proud Empire to fubjection.
Wild wrath will quickly fwell his haughty breaft,
Soon as he finds 'tis but a fhadowy blefling.——
'Twas fav'ring accident difcover'd to me

All

All that I know; this Evening as I ftood
Alone, retir'd, in the ftill gallery,
That leads up to th' appartment of my Brother,
T' indulge my melancholy thoughts,—

KING.

Proceed—

VARDANES.

A wretch approach'd with wary ftep, his eye
Spoke half his tale, denoting villany.
In hollow murmurs thus he queftion'd me.
Was I the Prince?—I anfwer'd to content him—
Then in his hand he held this paper forth.
" Take this, fays he, this *Bethas* greets thee with,
" Keep but your word our plot will meet fuccefs."
I fnatch'd it with more rafhnefs than difcretion,
Which taught him his miftake. In hafte he drew,
And aim'd his dagger at my breaft, but paid
His life, a forfeit, for his bold prefuming.

KING.

O Villain! Villain!

VARDANES.

Here, read this, my Lord—
I read it, and cold horror froze my blood,
And fhook me like an ague.

KING.

KING.

Ha!—what's this?—
" Doubt not Arabia's aid, fet me but free,
" I'll eafy pafs on the old cred'lous King,
" For fair *Evanthe's* Father."—Thus to atoms—
Oh! could I tear thefe curfed traitors thus.

{ Tears the paper
into pieces.]

VARDANES.

Curfes avail you nothing, he has pow'r,
And may abufe it to your prejudice.

KING.

I am refolv'd—

VARDANES.

Tho' Pris'ner in his camp,
Yet, *Bethas* was attended like a Prince,
As tho' he ftill commanded the Arabians.
'Tis true, when they approach'd the royal city,
He threw him into chains to blind our eyes,
A fhallow artifice—

KING.

That is a Truth.

VARDANES.

And, yet, he is your Son.

KING

KING.

Ah! that indeed—

VARDANES.

Why that ſtill heightens his impiety,
To ruſh to empire thro' his Father's blood,
And, in return of life, to give him death.

KING.

Oh! I am all on fire, yes I muſt tear
Theſe folds of venom from me.

VARDANES.

Sure 'twas *Lyſias*
That croſs'd the paſſage now.

KING.

'Tis to my wiſh.
I 'll in, and give him orders to arreſt
My traitor Son and *Bethas*—Now *Vardanes*
Indulge thy Father in this one requeſt—
Seize, with ſome horſe, *Evanthe*, and bear her
To your command—Oh! I 'll own my weakneſs—
I love with fondneſs mortal never knew—
Not Jove himſelf, when he forſook his heav'n,
And in a brutal ſhape diſgrac'd the God,
E'er lov'd like me.

VARDANES.

I will obey you, Sir.

Z   SCENE

SCENE IX.

VARDANES, alone.

I'll feize her, but I'll keep her for myfelf,
It were a fin to give her to his age—
To twine the blooming garland of the fpring
Around the faplefs trunks of wither'd oaks—
The night, methinks, grows ruder than it was,
Thus fhould it be, thus nature fhould be fhock'd,
And Prodigies, affrighting all mankind,
Foretell the dreadful bufinefs I intend.
The earth fhould gape, and fwallow cities up,
Shake from their haughty heights afpiring tow'rs,
And level mountains with the vales below;
The Sun amaz'd fhould frown in dark eclipfe,
And light retire to its unclouded heav'n;
While darknefs, burftirg from her deep recefs,
Should wrap all nature in eternal night.—
Ambition, glorious fever of the mind,
'Tis that which raifes us above mankind;
The fhining mark which bounteous heav'n has gave,
From vulgar fouls diftinguifhing the brave.

END of the THIRD ACT.

❀❀❀❀❀❀❀❀❀❀❀❀❀❀❀❀❀❀❀❀❀

ACT IV.   *SCENE* I.

A PRISON.

GOTARZES and PHRAATES.

PHRAATES.

Oh! fly my Prince, for fafety dwells not here,
    Hence let me urge thy flight with eager hafte,
Laft night thy Father figh'd his foul to blifs,
Bafe murther'd—

GOTARZES.
Murther'd? ye Gods!—

PHRAATES.
Alas! 'tis true.
Stabb'd in his flumber by a traitor's hand;
I fcarce can fpeak it—horror choaks my words——
Lyfias it was who did the damned deed,
Urg'd by the bloody Queen, and his curs'd rage,
Becaufe the King, thy Sire, in angry mood,
Once ftruck him on his foul difhoneft cheek.
Sufpicion gave me fears of this, when firft
I heard, the Prince, *Arfaces*, was imprifon'd;
By fell *Vardanes*' viles.

Z 2

GOTARZES.

GOTARZES.

Oh! horror! horror!
Hither I came to fhare my Brother's forrows,
To mingle tears, and give him figh for figh;
But this is double, double weight of woe.

PHRAATES.

'Tis held as yet a fecret from the world,
Frighted by hideous dreams I fhook off fleep,
And as I mus'd the garden walks along,
Thro' the deep gloom, clofe in a neighb'ring walk,
Vardanes with proud *Lyfias* I beheld,
Still eager in difcourfe they faw not me,
For yet the early dawn had not appear'd;
I fought a fecret ftand, where hid from view,
I heard ftern *Lyfias*, hail the Prince *Vardanes*
As Parthia's dreaded Lord—" 'Tis done, he cry'd,
" 'Tis done, and *Artabanus* is no more.
" The blow he gave me is repay'd in blood;
" Now fhall the morn behold two rifing funs:
" *Vardanes* thou, our better light, fhalt bring
" Bright day and joy to ev'ry heart."

GOTARZES.

Why flept
Your vengeance, oh! ye righteous Gods?

PHRAATES.

PHRAATES.

Then told

A tale, so fill'd with bloody circumstance,
Of this damn'd deed, that stiffen'd me with horror.
Vardanes seem'd to blame the hasty act,
As rash, and unadvis'd, by passion urg'd,
Which never yields to cool reflection's place.
But, being done, resolv'd it secret, least
The multitude should take it in their wise
Authority to pry into his death.
Arsaces was, by assassination,
Doom'd to fall. Your name was mention'd also—
But hurried by my fears away, I left
The rest unheard—

GOTARZES.

What can be done?—Reflection, why wilt thou
Forsake us, when distress is at our heels?
Phraates help me, aid me with thy council.

PHRAATES.

Then stay not here, fly to *Barzaphernès*,
His conqu'ring troops are at a trivial distance;
Soon will you reach the camp; he lov'd your Brother,
And your Father with affection serv'd; haste
Your flight, whilst yet I have the city-guard,
For *Lysias* I expect takes my command.
I to the camp dispatch'd a trusty slave,

Before

Before the morn had ſpread her bluſhing veil.
Away, you'll meet the Gen'ral on the road,
On ſuch a cauſe as this he'll not delay.

GOTARZES,

I thank your love—

SCENE II.

PHRAATES, alone.

I'll wait behind, my ſtay
May aid the cauſe; diſſembling I muſt learn,
Neceſſity ſhall teach me how to vary
My features to the looks of him I ſerve.
I'll thruſt myſelf diſguis'd among the croud,
And fill their ears with murmurs of the deed:
Whiſper all is not well, blow up the ſparks
Of diſcord, and it ſoon will flame to rage.

SCENE III.

QUEEN and LYSIAS.

QUEEN.

Haſte, and ſhew me to the Prince *Arſaces*,
Delay not, ſee the ſignet of *Vardanes*.

LYSIAS.

LYSIAS.

Royal *Thermusa*, why this eagerness?
This tumult of the soul?—what means this dagger?
Ha!—I suspect—

QUEEN.

Hold—for I'll tell thee, *Lysias.*
'Tis—oh! I scarce can speak the mighty joy—
I shall be greatly blest in dear revenge,
'Tis vengeance on *Arsaces*—yes, this hand
Shall urge the shining poniard to his heart,
And give him death—yea, give the ruffian death;
So shall I smile on his keen agonies.

LYSIAS.

Ha! am I robb'd of all my hopes of vengeance,
Shall I then calmly stand with all my wrongs,
And see another bear away revenge?

QUEEN.

For what can *Lysias* ask revenge, to bar
His Queen of hers?

LYSIAS.

Was I not scorn'd, and spurn'd,
With haughty insolence? like a base coward
Refus'd what e'er I ask'd, and call'd a boaster?
My honour sullied, with opprobrious words,

Which

Which can no more its former brightnefs know,
'Til, with his blood, I 've wafh'd the ftains away.
Say, fhall I then not feek for glorious vengeance?

QUEEN.

And what is this, to the fad Mother's griefs,
Her hope cut off, rais'd up with pain and care?
Hadſt thou e'er fupported the lov'd Prattler?
Hadſt thou like me hung o'er his infancy,
Wafting in wakeful mood the tedious night,
And watch'd his fickly couch, far mov'd from reft,
Waiting his health's return?—Ah! hadſt thou known
The parent's fondnefs, rapture, toil and forrow,
The joy his actions gave, and the fond wifh
Of fomething yet to come, to blefs my age,
And lead me down with pleafure to the grave,
Thou wouldſt not thus talk lightly of my wrongs.
But I delay——

LYSIAS.

To thee I then fubmit.
Be fure to wreck a double vengeance on him;
If that thou knowſt a part in all his body,
Where pain can moft be felt, ftrike, ftrike him there—
And let him know the utmoft height of anguifh.
It is a joy to think that he fhall fall,
Tho' 'tis another hand which gives the blow.

SCENE

SCENE IV.

ARSACES and BETHAS.

ARSACES.

Why should I linger out my joyless days,
When length of hope is length of misery?
Hope is a coz'ner, and beguiles our cares,
Cheats us with empty shews of happiness,
Swift fleeting joys which mock the faint embrace;
We wade thro' ills pursuing of the meteor,
Yet are distanc'd still.

BETHAS.

            Ah! talk not of hope——
Hope fled when bright *Astræa* spurn'd this earth,
And sought her seat among the shining Gods;
Despair, proud tyrant, ravages my breast,
And makes all desolation.

ARSACES.

How can I
Behold those rev'rent sorrows, see those cheeks
Moist with the dew which falls from thy sad eyes,
Nor imitate distraction's frantic tricks,
And chace cold lifeless reason from her throne?
I am the fatal cause of all this sorrow,

The

The ſpring of ills,—to know me is unhappineſs;—
And mis'ry, like a hateful plague, purſues
My wearied ſteps, and blaſts the ſpringing verdure.

BETHAS.

No;—It is I that am the ſource of all,
It is my fortune ſinks you to this trouble;
Before you ſhower'd your gentle pity on me,
You ſhone the pride of this admiring world.——
Evanthe ſprings from me, whoſe fatal charms
Produces all this ruin —Hear me heav'n!
If to another love ſhe ever yields,
And ſtains her ſoul with ſpotted falſehood's crime,
If e'en in expectation taſtes a bliſs,
Nor joins *Arſaces* with it, I will wreck
My vengeance on her, ſo that ſhe ſhall be
A dread example to all future times.

ARSACES.

Oh! curſe her not, nor threaten her with anger,
She is all gentleneſs, yet firm to truth,
And bleſt with ev'ry pleaſing virtue, free
From levity, her ſexes character.
She ſcorns to chace the turning of the wind,
Varying from point to point.

BETHAS.

I love her, ye Gods!

I need not speak the greatness of my love,
Each look which straining draws my soul to hers
Denotes unmeasur'd fondness; but 'mis'ry,
Like a fretful peevish child, can scarce tell
What it would wish, or aim at.

ARSACES.

Immortals, hear!
Thus do I bow my soul in humble pray'r——
Thou, King of beings, in whose breath is fate,
Show'r on *Evanthe* all thy choicest blessings,
And bless her with excess of happiness;
If yet, there is one bliss reserv'd in store,
And written to my name, oh! give it her,
And give me all her sorrows in return.

BETHAS.

'Rise, 'rise my Prince, this goodness o'erwhelms me,
She's too unworthy of so great a passion.

ARSACES.

I know not what it means, I'm not as usual,
Ill-boding cares, and restless fears oppress me,
And horrid dreams disturb, and fright, my slumbers;
But yesternight, 'tis dreadful to relate,
E'en now I tremble at my waking thoughts,
Methought, I stood alone upon the shore,
And, at my feet, there roll'd a sea of blood,

High

High wrought, and 'midft the waves, appear'd my Father,
Struggling for life; above him was *Vardanes*,
Pois'd in the air, he feem'd to rule the ftorm,
And, now and then, would pufh my Father down,
And for a fpace he'd fink beneath the waves,
And then, all gory, rife to open view,
His voice in broken accents reach'd my ear,
And bade me fave him from the bloody ftream;
Thro' the red billows eagerly I rufh'd,
But fudden woke, benum'd with chilling fear.

BETHAS.

Moft horrible indeed!—but let it pafs,
'Tis but the offspring of a mind difturb'd,
For forrow leaves impreffions on the fancy,
Which fhew moft fearful to us lock'd in fleep.

ARSACES.

Thermufa! ha!—what can be her defign?
She bears this way, and carries in her looks
An eagernefs importing violence.
Retire—for I would meet her rage alone.

SCENE V.

ARSACES and QUEEN.

ARSACES.

What means the proud *Thermufa* by this vifit,
Stoops heav'n-born pity to a breaft like thine?
Pity adorns th' virtuous, but ne'er dwells
Where hate, revenge, and rage diftract the foul.
Sure, it is hate that hither urg'd thy fteps,
To view misfortune with an eye of triumph.
I know thou lov'ft me not, for I have dar'd
To crofs thy purpofes, and, bold in cenfure,
Spoke of thy actions as they merited.
Befides, this hand 'twas flew the curs'd *Vonones.*

QUEEN.

And darft thou infolent to name *Vonones ?*
To heap perdition on thy guilty foul?
There needs not this to urge me to revenge—
But let me view this wonder of mankind,
Whofe breath can fet the buftling world in arms.
I fee no dreadful terrors in his eye,
Nor gathers chilly fears around my heart,
Nor ftrains my gazing eye with admiration,
And, tho' a woman, I can ftrike the blow.

ARSACES.

Aʀsᴀᴄᴇs.

Why gaze you on me thus? why hesitate?
Am I to die?

Qᴜᴇᴇɴ.

　　　　　Thou art—this dagger shall
Dissolve thy life, thy fleeting ghost I'll send
To wait *Vonones* in the shades below.

Aʀsᴀᴄᴇs.

And even there I'll triumph over him.

Qᴜᴇᴇɴ.

O, thou vile homicide! thy fatal hand
Has robb'd me of all joy; *Vonones*, to
Thy *Manes* this proud sacrifice I give.
That hand which sever'd the friendship of thy
Soul and body, shall never draw again
Imbitt'ring tears from sorr'wing mother's eyes.
This, with the many tears I've shed, receive—　　　[Offers to stab him]
Ha!—I'd strike; what holds my hand?—'tis n't pity.

Aʀsᴀᴄᴇs.

Nay, do not mock me, with the shew of death,
And yet deny the blessing; I have met
Your taunts with equal taunts, in hopes to urge
The blow with swift revenge; but since that fails,
I'll woo thee to compliance, teach my tongue

　　　　　　　　　　　　　　　Persuasion's

Perfuafion's winning arts, to gain thy foul;
I'll praife thy clemency, in dying accents
Blefs thee for, this, thy charitable deed.
Oh! do not ftand; fee, how my bofom heaves
To meet the ftroke; in pity let me die,
'Tis all the happinefs I now can know.

QUEEN.

How fweet the eloquence of dying men!
Hence Poets feign'd the mufic of the Swan,
When death upon her lays his icy hand,
She melts away in melancholy ftrains.

ARSACES.

Play not thus cruel with my poor requeft,
But take my loving Father's thanks, and mine.

QUEEN.

Thy Father cannot thank me now.

ARSACES.

He will,
Believe me, e'en whilft diffolv'd in ecftacy
On fond *Evanthe's* bofom, he will paufe,
One moment from his joys, to blefs the deed.

QUEEN.

What means this tumult in my breaft? from whence

Proceeds

Proceeds this fudden change? my heart beats high,
And foft compaffion makes me lefs than woman;
'll fearch no more for what I fear to know.

ARSACES.

Why drops the dagger from thy trembling hand?
Oh! yet be kind——

QUEEN.

        No: now I'd have thee live,
Since it is happinefs to die: 'Tis pain
That I would give thee, thus I bid thee live;
Yes, I would have thee a whole age a dying,
And fmile to fee thy ling'ring agonies.
All day I'd watch thee, mark each heighten'd pang,
While fpringing joy fhould fwell my panting bofom;
This I would have—But fhould this dagger give
Thy foul the liberty it fondly wifhes,
'Twould foar aloft, and mock my faint revenge.

ARSACES.

This mildnefs fhews moft foul, thy anger lovely.
Think that 'twas I who blafted thy fond hope,
Vonones now lies number'd with the dead,
And all your joys are buried in his grave;
My hand untimely pluck'd the precious flow'r,
Before its fhining beauties were difplay'd.

                                                QUEEN.

QUEEN.

O Woman! Woman! where's thy refolution?
Where's thy revenge? Where's all thy hopes of vengeance?
Giv'n to the winds—Ha! is it pity?—No————
I fear it wears another fofter name.
I'll think no more, but rufh to my revenge,
In fpite of foolifh fear, or woman's foftnefs;
Be_ fteady now my foul to thy refolves.
Yes, thou fhalt die, thus, on thy breaft, I write
Thy inftant doom—ha!—ye Gods !   {Queen ftarts, as, in great
                                       {fright, at hearing fomething]

ARSACES.

Why this paufe ?
Why doft thou idly ftand like imag'd vengeance,
With harmlefs terrors threatning on thy brow,
With lifted arm, yet canft not ftrike the blow ?

QUEEN.

It furely was the Echo to my fears,
The whiftling wind, perhaps, which mimick'd voice;
But thrice methought it loudly cry'd, "forbear."
Imagination hence—I'll heed thee not—

[Ghoft of *Artabanus* rifes]

Save me—oh!—fave me—ye eternal pow'rs!————
See!—fee it comes, furrounded with dread terrors————
Hence—hence! nor blaft me with that horrid fight————
Throw off that fhape, and fearch th' infernal rounds
For horrid forms, there's none can fhock like thine.

B b   GHOST

GHOST.

No; I will ever wear this form, thus e'er
Appear before thee; glare upon thee thus,
'Til desperation, join'd to thy damn'd crime,
Shall wind thee to the utmost height of frenzy.
In vain you grasp the dagger in your hand,
In vain you dress your brows in angry frowns,
In vain you raise your threatning arm in air,
Secure, *Arsaces* triumphs o'er your rage.
Guarded by fate, from thy accurs'd revenge,
Thou canst not touch his life; the Gods have giv'n
A softness to thy more than savage soul
Before unknown, to aid their grand designs.
Fate yet is lab'ring with some great event,
But what must follow I'm forbid to broach——
Think, think of me, I sink to rise again,
To play in blood before thy aking sight,
And shock thy guilty soul with hell-born horrors——
Think, think of *Artabanus!* and despair——   [Sinks]

QUEEN.

Think of thee, and despair?—yes, I'll despair——
Yet stay,—oh! stay, thou messenger of fate!
Tell me—Ha! 'tis gone—and left me wretched——

ARSACES.

Your eyes seem fix'd upon some dreadful object,
Horror and anguish cloath your whiten'd face,

                                            And

And your frame ſhakes with terror; I hear you ſpeak
As ſeeming earneſt in diſcourſe, yet hear
No ſecond voice.

QUEEN.

What! ſaw'ſt thou nothing?

ARSACES.

Nothing.

QUEEN.

Nor hear'd?——

ARSACES.

Nor hear'd.

QUEEN.

Amazing ſpectacle!——
Cold moiſt'ning dews diſtil from ev'ry pore,
I tremble like to palſied age—Ye Gods!
Would I could leave this loath'd deteſted being!—
Oh! all my brain's on fire—I rave! I rave!—   [Ghoſt riſes again]
Ha! it comes again—ſee, it glides along—
See, ſee, what ſtreams of blood flow from its wounds!
A crimſon torrent—Shield me, oh! ſhield me, heav'n.——

ARSACES.

Great, and righteous Gods!—

QUEEN.

QUEEN.

Ah! frown not on me—
Why doſt thou ſhake thy horrid locks at me?
Can I give immortality?—'tis gone—   [Ghoſt ſinks]
It flies me, ſee, ah!—ſtop it, ſtop it, haſte—

ARSACES.

Oh, piteous ſight!—

QUEEN.

Hiſt! prithee hiſt!—oh death!
I'm all on fire—now freezing bolts of ice
Dart thro' my breaſt—Oh! burſt ye cords of life——
Ha! who are ye?—Why do ye ſtare upon me?—
Oh!—defend me, from theſe bick'ring Furies!

ARSACES.

Alas! her ſenſe is loſt, diſtreſsful Queen!

QUEEN.

Help me, thou King of Gods! oh! help me! help!—
See! they envir'n me round—*Vonones* too,
The foremoſt leading on the dreadful troop—
But there, *Vardanes* beck'ns me to ſhun
Their helliſh rage—I come, I come!
Ah! they purſue me, with a ſcourge of fire.—

                                    [Runs out diſtracted.]

SCENE

SCENE VI.

ARSACES, alone.

Oh!—horror!—on the ground she breathless lies,
Silent, in death's cold sleep; the wall besmear'd
With brains and gore the marks of her despair.
O guilt! how dreadful dost thou ever shew!
How lovely are the charms of innocence!
How beauteous tho' in sorrows and distress!—
Ha!—what noise?— [Clashing of swords]

SCENE VII.

ARSACES, BARZAPHERNES and GOTARZES.

BARZAPHERNES.

At length we've forc'd our entrance—
O my lov'd Prince! to see thee thus, indeed,
Melts e'en me to a woman's softness; see
My eyes o'erflow—Are these the ornaments
For Royal hands? rude manacles! oh shameful!
Is this thy room of state, this gloomy goal?
Without attendance, and thy bed the pavement?
But, ah! how diff'rent was our parting last!
When flush'd with vict'ry, reeking from the slaughter,

You

You faw Arabia's Sons fcour o'er the plain
In fhameful flight, before your conqu'ring fword;
Then fhone you like the God of battle.

ARSACES.

Welcome !—
Welcome, my loyal friends ! *Barzaphernes!*
My good old foldier, to my bofom thus !
Gotarzes, my lov'd Brother ! now I'm happy.—
But, fay, my foldier, why thefe threatning arms?
Why am I thus releas'd by force? my Father,
I fhould have faid the King, had he relented,
He'd not have us'd this method to enlarge me.
Alas ! I fear, too forward in your love,
You'll brand me with the rebel's hated name.

BARZAPHERNES.

I am by nature blunt—the foldier's manner.
Unus'd to the foft arts practis'd at courts.
Nor can I move the paffions, or difguife
The forr'wing tale to mitigate the fmart.
Then feek it not: I would found the alarm,
Loud as the trumpet's clangour, in your ears;
Nor will I hail you, as our Parthia's King,
'Til you've full reveng'd your Father's murther.

ARSACES.

Murther?—good heav'n !

BARZAPHERNES.

BARZAPHERNES.

The tale requires fome time;
And opportunity muft not be loft;
Your traitor Brother, who ufurps your rights,
Muft, 'ere his faction gathers to a head,
Have from his brows his new-born honours torn.

ARSACES.

What, doft thou fay, murther'd by *Vardanes*?
Impious parricide!—detefted villain!—
Give me a fword, and onward to the charge,
Stop gufhing tears, for I will weep in blood,
And forrow with the groans of dying men.—
Revenge! revenge!—oh!—all my foul's on fire!

GOTARZES.

'Twas not *Vardanes* ftruck the fatal blow,
Though, great in pow'r ufurp'd, he dares fupport
The actor, vengeful *Lyfias*; to his breaft
He clafps, with grateful joy, the bloody villain;
Who foon meant, with ruffian wiles, to cut
You from the earth, and alfo me.

ARSACES.

Juft heav'ns!—
But, gentle Brother, how didft thou elude
The vigilant, fufpicious, tyrant's craft.

GOTARZES.

GOTARZES.

Phraates, by an accident, obtain'd
The knowledge of the deed, and warn'd by him
I bent my flight toward the camp, to feek
Protection and revenge; but fcarce I'd left
The city when I o'ertook the Gen'ral.

BARZAPHERNES.

'Ere the fun 'rofe I gain'd th' intelligence:
The foldiers when they heard the dreadful tale,
Firft ftood aghaft, and motionlefs with horror.
Then fuddenly, infpir'd with noble rage,
Tore up their enfigns, calling on their leaders
To march them to the city inftantly.
I, with fome trufty few, with fpeed came forward,
To raife our friends within, and gain your freedom.
Nor hazard longer, by delays, your fafety.
Already faithful *Phraates* has gain'd
A num'rous party of the citizens;
With thefe we mean t' attack the Royal Palace,
Crufh the bold tyrant with furprize, while funk
In falfe fecurity; and vengeance wreck,
'Ere that he thinks the impious crime be known.

ARSACES.

O! parent being, Ruler of yon heav'n!
Who bade creation fpring to order, hear me.

What

What ever fins are laid upon my foul,
Now let them not prove heavy on this day,
To fink my arm, or violate my caufe.
The facred rights of Kings, my Country's wrongs,
The punifhment of fierce impiety,
And a lov'd Father's death, call forth my fword.——

   Now on; I feel all calm within my breaft,
And ev'ry bufy doubt is hufh'd to reft;
Smile heav'n propitious on my virtuous caufe,
Nor aid the wretch who dares difdain your laws.

END of the FOURTH ACT.

ACT V. *SCENE* I.

The PALACE.

The Curtain rifes, flowly, to foft mufic, and difcovers *Evanthe* fleeping on a Sofa; after the mufic ceafes, *Vardanes* enters.

VARDANES.

NOW fhining Empire ftanding at the goal,
  Beck'ns me forward to increafe my fpeed;
But, yet, *Arfaces* lives, bane to my hopes,
Lyfias I'll urge to eafe me of his life,
Then give the villain up to punifhment.
The fhew of juftice gains the changeling croud.
Befides, I ne'er will harbour in my bofom
Such ferpents, ever ready with their flings——
But now one hour for love and fair *Evanthe*——
Hence with ambition's cares——fee, where reclin'd,
In flumbers all her forrows are difmifs'd,
Sleep feems to heighten ev'ry beauteous feature,
And adds peculiar foftnefs to each grace.
She weeps——in dreams fome lively forrow pains her——
I'll take one kifs——oh! what a balmy fweetnefs!
Give me another——and another ftill——
For ever thus I'd dwell upon her lips.

Re

Be still my heart, and calm unruly transports.——
Wake her, with music, from this mimic death.   [Music sounds]

SONG.

Tell me, Phillis, tell me why,
   You appear so wond'rous coy,
When that glow, and sparkling eye,
   Speak you want to taste the joy?
Prithee give this fooling o'er,
Nor torment your lover more.

While youth is warm within our veins,
   And nature tempts us to be gay,
Give to pleasure loose the reins,
   Love and youth fly swift away.
Youth in pleasure should be spent,
Age will come, we'll then repent.

EVANTHE (waking)

I come ye lovely shades—Ha! am I here?
Still in the tyrant's palace? Ye bright pow'rs!
Are all my blessings then but vis'onary?
Methought I was arriv'd on that blest shore
Where happy souls for ever dwell, crown'd with
Immortal bliss; *Arsaces* led me through
The flow'ry groves, while all around me gleam'd
Thousand and thousand shades, who welcom'd me
With pleasing songs of joy—*Vardanes*, ha!—

VARDANES.

Why beams the angry lightning of thine eye
Againſt thy ſighing ſlave? Is love a crime?
Oh! if to dote, with ſuch exceſs of paſſion
As riſes e'en to mad extravagance
Is criminal, I then am ſo, indeed.

EVANTHE.

Away! vile man!—

VARDANES.

If to purſue thee e'er
With all the humbleſt offices of love,
If ne'er to know one ſingle thought that does
Not bear thy bright idea, merits ſcorn—

EVANTHE.

Hence from my ſight—nor let me, thus, pollute
Mine eyes, with looking on a wretch like thee,
Thou cauſe of all my ills; I ſicken at
Thy loathſome preſence—

VARDANES.

'Tis not always thus,
Nor doſt thou ever meet the ſounds of love
With rage and fierce diſdain: *Arſaces*, ſoon,
Could ſmooth thy brow, and melt thy icy breaſt.

EVANTHE.

EVANTHE.

Ha! does it gall thee ? Yes, he could, he could;
Oh! when he fpeaks, fuch fweetnefs dwells upon
His accents, all my foul diffolves to love,
And warm defire; fuch truth and beauty join'd!
His looks are foft and kind, fuch gentlenefs
Such virtue fwells his bofom! in his eye
Sits majefty, commanding ev'ry heart.
Strait as the pine, the pride of all the grove,
More blooming than the fpring, and fweeter far,
Than afphodels or rofes infant fweets.
Oh! I could dwell forever on his praife,
Yet think eternity was fcarce enough
To tell the mighty theme; here in my breaft
His image dwells, but one dear thought of him,
When fancy paints his Perfon to my eye,
As he was wont in tendernefs diffolv'd,
Sighing his vows, or kneeling at my feet,
Wipes off all mem'ry of my wretchednefs.

VARDANES.

I know this brav'ry is affected, yet
It gives me joy, to think my rival only
Can in imagination tafte thy beauties.
Let him,—'twill eafe him in his folitude,
And gild the horrors of his prifon-houfe,
Till death fhall——

EVANTHE.

EVANTHE.

      Ha! what was that? till death—ye Gods!
Ah, now I feel diſtreſs's tort'ring pang——
Thou canſt not villain—darſt not think his death—
O mis'ry!—

VARDANES.

      Naught but your kindneſs ſaves him,
Yet bleſs me, with your love, and he is ſafe;
But the ſame frown which kills my growing hopes,
Gives him to death.

EVANTHE.

      O horror, I could die
Ten thouſand times to ſave the lov'd *Arſaces*.
Teach me the means, ye pow'rs, how to ſave him:
Then lead me to what ever is my fate.

VARDANES.

Not only ſhall he die, but to thy view
I'll bring the ſcene, thoſe eyes that take delight
In cruelty, ſhall have enough of death.
E'en here, before thy ſight, he ſhall expire,
Not ſudden, but by ling'ring torments; all
That miſchief can invent ſhall be practis'd
To give him pain; to lengthen out his woe
I'll ſearch around the realm for ſkillful men,
To find new tortures.

                        EVANTHE.

EVANTHE.

Oh! wrack not thus my foul!

VARDANES.

The fex o'erflows with various humours, he
Who catches not their fmiles the very moment,
Will lofe the bleffing—I'll improve this foftnefs.——   [Afide]
——Heav'n never made thy beauties to deftroy,   [to her]
They were to blefs, and not to blaft mankind;
Pity fhould dwell within thy lovely breaft,
That facred temple ne'er was form'd for hate
A habitation; but a refidence
For love and gaiety.

EVANTHE.

Oh! heav'ns!

VARDANES.

That figh,
Proclaims your kind confent to fave *Arfaces*.   [Laying hold of her]

EVANTHE.

Ha! villain, off—unhand me—hence—

VARDANES.

In vain
Is opportunity to thofe, who fpend
An idle courtfhip on the fair, they well
                                        Deferve

Deferve their fate, if they 're difdain'd;—her charms
To rufh upon, and conquer oppofition,
Gains the Fair one's praife; an active lover
Suits, who lies afide the coxcomb's empty whine,
And forces her to blifs.

EVANTHE.

Ah! hear me, hear me,
Thus kneeling, with my tears, I do implore thee:
Think on my innocence, nor force a joy
Which will ever fill thy foul with anguifh.
Seek not to load my ills with infamy,
Let me not be a mark for bitter fcorn,
To bear proud virtue's taunts and mocking jeers.
And like a flow'r, of all its fweetnefs robb'd,
Be trod to earth, neglected and difdain'd,
And fpurn'd by ev'ry vulgar faucy foot.

VARDANES.

Speak, fpeak forever—mufic's in thy voice,
Still attentive will I liften to thee,
Be hufh'd as night, charm'd with the magic found.

EVANTHE.

Oh! teach me, heav'n, foft moving eloquence,
To bend his ftubborn foul to gentlenefs.—
Where is thy virtue? Where thy princely luftre?

Ah!

Ah! wilt thou meanly ftoop to do a wrong,
And ftain thy honour with fo foul a blot?
Thou who fhouldft be a guard to innocence.
Leave force to brutes—for pleafure is not found
Where ftill the foul's averfe; horror and guilt,
Diftraction, defperation chace her hence.
Some happier gentle Fair one you may find;
Whofe yielding heart may bend to meet your flame,
In mutual love foft joys alone are found;
When fouls are drawn by fecret fympathy,
And virtue does on virtue fmile.

VARDANES.

No more——
Her heav'nly tongue will charm me from th' intent——
Hence coward foftnefs, force fhall make me bleft.

EVANTHE.

Affift me, ye blefs't pow'rs!—oh! ftrike, ye Gods!
Strike me, with thunder dead, this moment, e'er
I fuffer violation——

VARDANES.

'Tis in vain,
The idle pray'rs by fancy'd grief put up,
Are blown by active winds regardlefs by;
Nor ever reach the heav'ns.

D d

SCENE

SCENE II.

VARDANES, EVANTHE, and LYSIAS.

LYSIAS.
Arm, arm, my Lord!——

VARDANES.
Damnation! why this interruption now?——

LYSIAS.
Oh! arm! my noble Prince, the foe's upon us.
Arſaces, by *Barzaphernes* releas'd,
Join'd with the citizens, aſſaults the Palace,
And ſwears revenge for *Artabanus'* death.

VARDANES.
Ha! what? revenge for *Artabanus'* death?——
'Tis the curſe of Princes that their counſels,
Which ſhould be kept like holy myſteries,
Can never reſt in ſilent ſecrecy.
Fond of employ, ſome curſed tattling tongue
Will ſtill divulge them.

LYSIAS.
Sure ſome fiend from hell,

In

In mifchief eminent, to crofs our views,
Has giv'n th' intelligence, for man could not,

EVANTHE.

Oh ! ever bleft event !—All-gracious heav'n !
This beam of joy revives me.

SCENE III.

VARDANES, EVANTHE, LYSIAS, to them, an OFFICER.

OFFICER.
Hafte ! my Lord !
Or all will foon be loft; tho' thrice repuls'd
By your e'erfaithful guards, they ftill return
With double fury.

VARDANES.
Hence, then, idle love——
Come forth, my trufty fword—curs'd misfortune !—
Had I but one fhort hour, without relu&ance,
I'd meet them, tho' they brib'd the pow'rs of hell,
To place their furies in the van: Yea, rufh
To meet this dreadful Brother 'midft the war—
Hafte to the combat—Now a crown or death—
The wretch who dares to give an inch of ground
Till I retire, fhall meet the death he fhun'd.
Away—away! delays are dang'rous now—

D d 2   SCENE.

SCENE IV.

EVANTHE, alone.

Now heav'n be partial to *Arsaces* cause,
Nor leave to giddy chance when virtue strives;
Let victory fit on his warlike helm,
For juſtice draws his ſword : be thou his aid,
And let the oppoſer's arm ſink with the weight
Of his moſt impious crimes—be ſtill my heart,
For all that thou canſt aid him with is pray'r.
Oh! that I had the ſtrength of thouſands in me!
Or that my voice could wake the ſons of men
To join, and cruſh the tyrant!—

SCENE V.

EVANTHE and CLEONE.

EVANTHE.

My *Cleone*—
Welcome thou partner of my joys and ſorrows.

CLEONE.

Oh! yonder terror triumphs uncontroul'd,
And glutton death ſeems never ſatisfy'd.

Each

Each soft senfation loft in thoughtlefs rage,
And breaft to breaft, oppos'd in furious war,
The fiery Chiefs receive the vengeful fteel.
O'er lifelefs heaps of men the foldiers climb
Still eager for the combat, while the ground
Made flipp'ry by the gufhing ftreams of gore
Is treach'rous to their feet.—Oh! horrid fight !—
Too much for me to ftand, my life was chill'd,
As from the turret I beheld the fight,
It forc'd me to retire.

EVANTHE.

What of *Arfaces?*

CLEONE.

I faw him active in the battle, now,
Like light'ning, piercing thro' the thickeft foe,
Then fcorning to difgrace his fword in low
Plebeian blood—loud for *Vardanes* call'd—
To meet him fingly, and decide the war.

EVANTHE.

Save him, ye Gods !—oh! all my foul is fear—
Fly, fly *Cleone,* to the tow'r again,
See how fate turns the ballance; and purfue
Arfaces with thine eye; mark ev'ry blow,
Obferve if fome bold villain dares to urge
His fword prefumptuous at my Hero's breaft.
Hafte, my *Cleone,* hafte, to eafe my fears.

SCENE

SCENE VI.

EVANTHE, alone.

Ah!—what a cruel torment is fufpenfe!
My anxious foul is torn 'twixt love and fear,
Scarce can I pleafe me with one fancied blifs
Which kind imagination forms, but reafon,
Proud, furly reafon, fnatches the vain joy,
And gives me up again to fad diftrefs.
Yet I can die, and fhould *Arfaces* fall
This fatal draught fhall eafe me of my forrrows.

SCENE VII.

CLEONE, alone.

Oh! horror! horror! horror!—cruel Gods!—
I faw him fall—I did—pierc'd thro' with wounds—
Curs'd! curs'd *Vardanes!*—hear'd the gen'ral cry,
Which burft, as tho' all nature had diffolv'd.
Hark! how they fhout! the noife feems coming this way.

SCENE

SCENE VIII.

ARSACES, GOTARZES, BARZAPHERNES and OFFICERS, with
VARDANES and LYSIAS, prifoners.

ARSACES.

Thanks to the ruling pow'rs who bleſt our arms,
Prepare the facrifices to the Gods,
And grateful fongs of tributary praiſe.———
Gotarzes, fly, my Brother, find *Evanthe*,
And bring the lovely mourner to my arms.

GOTARZES.

Yes, I'll obey you, with a willing fpeed.   [*Exit Gotarzes*]

ARSACES.

Thou, *Lyſias*, from yon tow'r's afpiring height
Be hurl'd to death, thy impious hands are ſtain'd
With royal blood————Let the traitor's body
Be giv'n to hungry dogs.

LYSIAS.

Welcome grim death!————
I've fed thy maw with Kings, and lack no more
Revenge—Now, do thy duty Officer.

OFFICER.

Yea, and would lead all traitors gladly. thus,—
The boon of their deferts.

SCENE

SCENE IX.

ARSACES, VARDANES, BARZAPHERNES.

ARSACES.
But for *Vardanes*,
The Brother's name forgot——

VARDANES.

You need no more,
I know the reft—Ah! death is near, my wounds
Permit me not to live—my breath grows fhort,
Curs'd be *Phraates* arm which ftop'd my fword,
Ere it had reach'd thy proud exulting heart.
But the wretch paid dear for his prefuming;
A juft reward.——

ARSACES.

He finks, yet bear him up——

VARDANES.

Curs'd be the multitude which o'erpow'r'd me,
And beat me to the ground, cover'd with wounds—
But, oh! 'tis done! my ebbing life is done—
I feel death's hand upon me—Yet, I die
Juft as I wifh, and daring for a crown,
Life without rule is my difdain; I fcorn

To fwell a haughty Brother's fneaking train,
To wait upon his ear with flatt'ring tales,
And court his fmiles; come, death, in thy cold arms,
Let me forget Ambition's mighty toil,
And fhun the triumphs of a hated Brother—
O! bear me off—Let not his eyes' enjoy
My agonies—My fight grows dim with death.   [They bear him off.]

SCENE the Laft.

ARSACES, GOTARZES, BARZAPHERNES, and EVANTHE fupported.

EVANTHE.

Lead me, oh! lead me, to my lov'd *Arfaces,*
Where is he?—

ARSACES.

Ha! what's this?—Juft heav'ns!—my fears——

EVANTHE.

Arfaces, oh! thus circl'd in thy arms,
I die without a pang.

ARSACES.

Ha! die?—why ftare ye,
Ye lifelefs ghofts? Have none of ye a tongue
To tell me I'm undone?

E e   GOTARZES.

GOTARZES.

Soon, my Brother,
Too foon, you'll know it by the fad effects;
And if my grief will yet permit my tongue
To do its office, thou fhalt hear the tale.
Cleone, from the turret, view'd the battle,
And on *Phraates* fix'd her erring fight,
Thy brave unhappy friend fhe took for thee,
By his garb deceiv'd, which like to thine he wore.
Still with her eye fhe follow'd him, where-e'er
He pierc'd the foe, and to *Vardanes* fword
She faw him fall a haplefs victim, then,
In agonies of grief, flew to *Evanthe*,
And told the dreadful tale—the fatal bowl
I faw——

ARSACES.

Be dumb, nor ever give again
Fear to the heart, with thy ill-boding voice.

EVANTHE.

Here, I'll reft, till death, on thy lov'd bofom,
Here let me figh my—Oh! the poifon works——

ARSACES.

Oh! horror!——

EVLNTHE.

Ceafe—this forrow pains me more

Than

Than all the wringing agonies of death,
The dreadful parting of the foul from, this,
Its wedded clay—Ah! there—that pang fhot thro'
My throbbing heart—

ARSACES.

   Save her, ye Gods!—oh! fave her!
And I will bribe ye with clouds of incenfe;
Such num'rous facrifices, that your altars
Shall even fink beneath the mighty load.

EVANTHE.

When I am dead, diffolv'd to native duft,
Yet let me live in thy dear mem'ry—
One tear will not be much to give *Evanthe.*

ARSACES.

My eyes fhall e'er two running fountains be,
And wet thy urn with everflowing tears,
Joy ne'er again within my breaft fhall find
A refidence—Oh! fpeak, once more—

EVANTHE.

   Life's juft out—
My Father—Oh! protect his honour'd age,
And give him fhelter from the ftorms of fate,
He's long been fortune's fport—Support me—Ah!—
I can no more—my glafs is fpent—farewel—
Forever—*Arfaces!*—Oh!   [Dies]

E e 2

ARSACES,

ARSACES.

Stay, oh! ſtay,
Or take me with thee—dead! ſhe's cold and dead!
Her eyes are clos'd, and all my joys are flown—
Now burſt ye elements, from your reſtraint,
Let order ceaſe, and chaos be again.
Break! break tough heart!—oh! torture—life diſſolve—
Why ſtand ye idle? Have I not one friend
To kindly free me from this pain? One blow,
One friendly blow would give me eaſe.

BARZAPHERNES.

The Gods
Forefend!—Pardon me, Royal Sir, if I
Dare, ſeemingly diſloyal, ſeize your ſword,
Deſpair may urge you far——

ARSACES.

Ha! traitors! rebels!——
Hoary rev'rend Villain! what, diſarm me?
Give me my ſword—what, ſtand ye by, and ſee
Your Prince inſulted? Are ye rebels all?—

BRAZAPHERNES.

Be calm, my gracious Lord!

GOTARZES.

Oh! my lov'd Brother!

ARSKCES.

ARSACES.

Gotarzes too! all! all! confpir'd againft me?
Still, are ye all refolv'd that I muft live,
And feel the momentary pangs of death?—
Ha!—this, fhall make a paffage for my foul—

              [Snatches *Barzaphernes'* fword.]

Out, out vile cares, from your diftrefs'd abode—   [Stabs himfelf.]

BARZAPHERNES.

Oh! ye eternal Gods!

GOTARZES.

      Diftraction! heav'ns!
I fhall run mad—

ARSACES.

      Ah! 'tis in vain to grieve—
The fteel has done its part, and I'm at reft.—
Gotarzes wear my crown, and be thou bleft,
Cherifh, *Barzaphernes*, my trufty chief—
I faint, oh! lay me by *Evanthe's* fide—
Still wedded in our death's—*Bethas*—

BARZAPHNERNES.

      Defpair,
My Lord, has broke his heart, I faw him ftretch'd,
Along the flinty pavement, in his gaol—
Cold, lifelefs——

                         ARSACES.

ARSACES.

He 's happy then—had he heard
This tale, he 'd—Ah! *Evanthe* chides my foul,
For ling'ring here fo long—another pang
And all the world, adieu—oh! adieu!—   [Dies]

GOTARZES.

Oh!—

Fix me, heav'n, immoveable, a ftatue,
And free me from o'erwhelming tides of grief.

BARZAPHERNES.

Oh! my lov'd Prince, I foon fhall follow thee;
Thy laurel'd glories whither are they fled?—
Would I had died before this fatal day!—
Triumphant garlands pride my foul no more,
No more the lofty voice of war can charm—
And why then am I here? Thus then—   [Offers to ftab himfelf]

GOTARZES.

Ah! hold,
Nor rafhly urge the blow—think of me, and
Live—My heart is wrung with ftreaming anguifh,
Tore with the fmarting pangs of woe, yet, will I
Dare to live, and ftem misfortune's billows.
Live then, and be the guardian of my youth,
And lead me on thro' virtue's rugged path.

Barzaphernes

BARZAPHERNES.

O, glorious youth, thy words have rous'd the
Drooping genius of my foul; thus, let me
Clafp thee, in my aged arms; yes, I will live—
Live, to fupport thee in thy kingly rights,
And when thou'rt firmly fix'd, my tafk's perform'd,
My honourable tafk—Then I'll retire,
Petition gracious heav'n to blefs my work,
And in the filent grave forget my cares.

GOTARZES.

Now, to the Temple, let us onward move,
And ftrive t' appeafe the angry pow'rs above.
Fate yet may have fome ills referv'd in ftore,
Continu'd curfes, to torment us more.
Tho', in their diftrict, Monarchs rule alone,
Jove fways the mighty Monarch on his throne:
Nor can the fhining honours which they wear,
Purchafe one joy, or fave them from one care.

FINIS.